Avalanche

Avalanche

M. Liz Boyle

M. Liz Boyle
Avalanche

© 2019 M. Liz Boyle

mlizboyle@gmail.com

Cover photo by iStock

Cover design © Giant Leap Design

Author photo by Krista Swanson/Simple Wonder Arts

First edition
ISBN 978-1-7334272-0-3
ISBN 978-1-7334272-1-0

Contents

Dear Reader,   2|6

Acknowledgements

Special thanks to my Father and His Son; my husband Dustin for sharing many adventures with me and encouraging me through this one, as well as explaining many mountaineering and rescue details to me; my parents for rooting for me; my wonderful beta reading team: James Guy III, Nia Flavin, Miranda Gibson, Hannah Gilmer, David Markopoulos, Cynthia Saladin, Jennifer Saladin, Abigail Shafer – your input means tons to me, and I greatly appreciate your help; my gracious and thorough editor Beth Jernberg; Krista Swanson for the fun photo shoot; Karen at the Woodville Library; Rollan and Maria Wengert for urging me to self-publish and answering various questions; David and Sarah Witt for their support and advice; Clara, Walker, Kelty and all of my beloved family members and friends – you all rock!

To adventure seekers everywhere, this story is for you.

1
___

As I felt the wall of snow crash into me and sweep me down the mountain like I was an autumn leaf, I would have given almost anything to take back my decision to go along with this reckless idea. When I first heard the roar, followed by a deep rumble and rushing sound, all I could do was scream. My big sister Ellie grabbed my hand and frantically told me to grab our little sister, Lydie. I desperately reached back for her, but where was she? She had been hiking just behind me, but apparently had slowed. Sawyer and Marshall Miles bounded through the deep snow to us. Sawyer, almost eighteen, hollered, "AVALANCHE! Run to the side of the ridge!" *Run to the side.* I had read that tip in an article a few months ago, but thinking about it seemed much more possible than actually sprinting through shin-deep snow with a mammoth mass thundering toward me.

"Where's Lydie?" Sawyer demanded.

"I don't know!" I cried.

Ellie and Sawyer exchanged a distressed glance, then took off together, amazingly reaching Lydie just before the snow mass roared into us.

"Swim uphill!" Marshall shouted. *Swim uphill.* I remembered Dad telling a story of a guy he knew from his mountaineering job that got caught in an avalanche and "swam" to stay toward the surface of the snow. I hysterically began flailing my arms and legs, certainly no Olympic stroke, but perhaps it resembled swimming enough to stay above the surface of the crashing snow. While swimming, I craned my head in every direction, trying to catch a glimpse – what I prayed would not be my last glimpse – of my dear sisters and Sawyer, but all I saw was white. Ominous, smothering white. And then black.

Black. Stifling black. Moments before, the full moon bounced enough light off the pure white snow to read a map. Now I was smothered in darkness. Was this a nightmare? I tried to roll over in my sleeping bag, but no, I wasn't in my sleeping bag. My whole body hurt. My face felt bruised. The memory flashed into mind, almost as quickly as the avalanche had hit us. Avalanche. Lydie! Ellie! The Miles boys! What was I doing here?? If I had followed my gut and refused to go on this hike, we would be safely asleep in our tent next to our parents' tent. Our parents' tent. Mom and Dad – oh, no! How would they cope with the news that their children had been in an avalanche? I had to get out. I would get out. God willing, I would do everything in my power to escape.

Panic surged through me. Instinctively, my body tried to thrash, tried desperately to get up, but I was stuck. The snow was packed so tightly that I could barely move my hands. Without thinking, I began to pray. At first, my plea was panicked, but gradually, I managed to calm down and really ask God for help.

Stay calm, I reminded myself again, and then mocked the thought of staying calm while drowning in snow. *Stop that. Think, Marlee. Oh yeah, when buried in the snow, first determine which way is down, then dig toward the opposite direction.* The snow was stiff, but not as stiff as I first thought, indicating to me that I must be near the surface. My left hand was near my face. After wiggling it for a few seconds I managed, with some difficulty, to get it to my mouth and I dug a small air pocket. Letting a drop of saliva onto my lip, I felt it fall down my left cheek. So gravity was left. *Dig to the right.* Slowly, I inched my hands to my right side and pushed snow away from my body. It took all of my strength to move the solid snow just a few inches. My breathing sped up again, partially due to fear and partially due to the workout of digging. Pausing to take a break, I wondered how long my pocket of air could provide enough oxygen. Then I heard my name. Or was that my imagination?

"Marlee!" It was definitely Marshall's voice. I tried to scream back to him, but my voice deafeningly echoed directly back to me in my cave. I felt a surge of relief knowing at least Marshall and I were alive; I begged God that the others were, too.

Three more energy-draining scoops with my arms, and I felt my right fingertips emerge. I wiggled them and suddenly felt as free as a butterfly bursting from a cocoon.

"Marlee!" I heard him shout again.

A few more frantic scoops, and I jerked my head out of the snow. "Marsh!" I hollered. He was about forty feet away and came running to me. He looked stunned and incredibly scared as he dug his gloved fingers into the snow around my head and grabbed my shoulders. He was breathing so hard that I thought he would give himself a headache.

"I thought I was the only one who made it," his face crumpled, and he let out a sob.

Marshall's emotions made me feel like crying, too. I mean, I'm a girl, so if I cry, it might not *actually* be a big deal. But even Marshall was crying! What had we just survived?! What was ahead of us? If we didn't make it back to camp before sunrise, our parents would be worried sick. Where were the others? Marshall said he thought he was the only one who had survived, so that meant that Lydie, Ellie and Sawyer were still missing. By now, tears were slowly sliding down my cheeks, and my nose was running. Marshall's head was bent low, but all at once, he lifted his head, looked at me, and began scooping snow from around my body. I was lying somewhat sideways, kind of parallel to the mountain.

"Can you unbuckle your pack?" Marshall asked me. With my right hand, I reached down and numbly unclipped my backpack's waist belt, then the sternum strap.

"Okay, I'm unbuckled, but I don't know that I can wriggle out of the shoulder straps. Moving in this snow is like swimming in a sea of cold peanut butter."

Marshall had scooped most of my right side free, and feeling like a stiff hippo, I heaved and sort of rolled out of my snowy cocoon, my pack still loosely on my back. My rib cage expanded dramatically, no longer confined in the dense snow. I gulped several huge breaths, just now realizing that I had been forced to take shallow breaths while buried. *Buried alive.* The thought made me very thankful to be out of the snow, but also very worried about the others. Marshall dropped to his knees next to me and again grabbed my shoulders. I looked back into the spot where I had been, and to my amazement it was barely below the surface. At first, when I had felt like I would never get out, I would have figured I was twenty feet down, not five inches.

"You okay?" Marshall stammered. Honestly, I felt better than he appeared, and I was afraid he was having a panic attack – just what we needed.

"Uh," I quickly thought, tested out my limbs, stood up and successfully took two steps, "I think so. What about you?"

"Oh Marlee, you're bleeding!" Marshall exclaimed.

"Where? *Are you okay?*" I demanded, his anxiety making me more nervous.

"Your forehead," he pointed, and I stretched my left hand up, noticing for the first time that my arm felt stiff after being packed under the snow, but with my glove on I couldn't feel how severe the bleeding was.

"I don't think I'm losing much blood, so if you're okay, I say we start searching for the rest of the group," I said, my voice sounding more confident than I felt.

I knew that avalanche victims have to get out ASAP, so I forced my emotions out of my mind. There wasn't time to worry and wonder. We had to find Sawyer, Ellie and Lydie. Marshall was still visibly distraught. He looked like I felt. But right now, we had to act.

This time it was me putting my hands on Marshall's shoulders. Suddenly feeling like a mother hen, I prayed that it would calm him enough to think clearly. "Marsh," I began, "we just lived through an *avalanche*." He nodded and his breathing began to regulate. "Right now," I continued, "our job is to search for the other three." His breathing began to increase. I kept my hands firmly on his shoulders. Marshall must have had an impressive growth spurt during the year, because last summer I was about four inches taller than he. Now, standing face to face, we matched each other for height. I bet Marshall clears out their fridge weekly!

"Marshall, you and I are going to stay together, side by side, and we are going to find our siblings. You know more about rescue than I do," I went on, thinking that delegating him a role would help him focus, "so tell me, where do you think they are?" When the words came out of my mouth, it sounded so devastating, as if they had hit, landed, and would remain until found. That's what they call 'search and recovery.' I silently begged God this would be a search and *rescue.* I again swallowed my fear and maintained eye contact with him.

"Well," he began matter-of-factly, "Sawyer and Ellie ran down the ridge as the avalanche hit. So I would say that we need to start searching about twenty feet lower than where you were buried."

I nodded, and without a word, I repositioned and buckled my pack before I noticed Marshall's was gone. "You lost your pack?" I quietly asked.

Marshall blankly nodded. His backpack had contained one of two first aid kits. The other was in Ellie's. "Well at least we still have gorp," I tried to lighten the mood, referring to the "good old raisins and peanuts" in my pack. My attempt at a joke was not appreciated, so I turned and we headed down the ridge, where he figured Sawyer and my sisters were. It had probably only been two minutes since I was dug out, but every minute under the snow made the situation more serious. Like, exponentially more serious.

"Look for any sign of them," Marshall said, "gloves, packs, headlamps," he trailed off. Glancing in the direction he faced, I nearly whooped for joy when I saw Lydie's glove. "Look!" I squealed. Together, we ran to her glove and began digging and calling her name. As I dug with my trowel, I wondered if we should spread out to increase our chances of finding her, but I sure didn't want to be alone right now, so I stayed close to Marshall. Suddenly I scooped into a pocket similar to the one I had dug in front of my mouth, and my heart raced with renewed vigor. Two more digs, more carefully now, and Lydie's beautiful, eleven-year-old face surfaced. "Lydie!" I sang, "Oh, Lydie, can you hear me? Does anything hurt?" Marshall, who had been digging a few feet downhill of me, ran to my side and began furiously digging around Lydie's face.

Lydie's eyes opened and she weakly smiled. I threw my arms around her head and whispered, "Thank You, God! Oh, Lydie, I love you." When I pulled my head away from hers, I noticed that her expression was weak.

"Get her out!" shouted Marshall, "She can't breathe! The pressure on her lungs is too much!"

I had been so happy to see Lydie's face that I had

momentarily forgotten that the rest of her was still cemented in the packed snow. Startled by Marshall's command, I reached along Lydie's side and wrapped my arms around her waist. Trying to do a squat, I heaved with all my might, hoping to pull Lydie up with me.

"Yeeowwww!!" she shrieked, the pain in her voice sounding authentic.

Startled, I staggered backward, falling onto the ground.

"Tell us what hurts, Lydie," Marshall directed her.

"Leg," she whimpered as she tried to blink away the tears that had begun gathering in her eyes and trickling down her face.

Marshall glanced at me, squinted his eyes to try to see her lower body in the semidarkness, and then looked back to me. His eyes were serious as he quietly said, "You stay by her face and calm her. Make sure she keeps breathing. Start clearing snow off her chest if you can. I'll work on digging out her legs."

"Hey, Lydie, how was your ride down the slope?" I tried to sound casual, hoping my nonchalant attitude would lighten everyone's thoughts. With the back of my glove, I gently wiped snow and tears off her eyelashes and face.

Her weak smile and sigh confirmed that she was in pain and very scared. I tilted her face to look squarely in her eyes, "Lydie," I started, sounding more confident than I was, "God has your back. We're here now, and we're going to do all we can to get back to Mom and Dad."

With that, a lone tear rolled down her cheek, which made my heart ache. Marshall winced, as if he had just now thought of our parents. As he dug deeper, I heard him gasp. Cautiously looking into the hole he was making, my throat felt like it caved in when I saw Lydie's left leg. Her boot was at knee level, and her lower leg was twisted away from her body.

That explains her pathetic, "Yeeowwww!!" when I first tried heaving her out of the avalanche, I thought. It made me hurt just looking at her disfigured ankle.

Marshall sharply sucked in a breath, and I was afraid he would go back into panic mode. Suddenly I thought I heard Ellie's voice, but it sounded distant, and Marshall and Lydie did not appear to have heard.

"Maybe," I said as the thought occurred to me, "now that Lydie can breathe, we should look for Sawyer and Ellie. Lydie's stable, but if the other two are still under the snow, we need to get them out ASAP."

Lydie faintly nodded. "Marlee's right, Marsh. You got me to air, so we can worry about my leg once we know Ellie and Sawyer are safe."

Marshall did not hesitate to jump up, and though I realized I should help him find the others, it was very hard to pull myself away from my injured little sister. "Do you have any idea where they are?" I asked her.

"Ellie was holding my right arm. Sawyer—"

But she was cut off by a voice shouting, "OVER HERE!" Marshall stopped walking, and loudly said, "Where are you?"

Then, like a dream, Sawyer jogged over to us, with Ellie a few strides behind. Like they were out for a midnight run. How did they look so normal? Since they obviously weren't buried, they must have made it to the side of the ridge before the avalanche hit. Sawyer was limping, but Ellie looked fine. I mean, scared out of her wits, but physically fine.

"Ellie! We're here! Everybody's accounted for now," I informed her. "Are you okay?"

Ellie and I fiercely hugged each other, and I suddenly felt much more confident with my seventeen-year-old sister here. And she still had her backpack. The backpack with the remaining first aid kit. *Phew.* Marshall gave his brother a manly-type slap on the shoulder and sighed, "Boy, is it good to see you."

"You too, Brother," Sawyer breathed, his hands on his knees. "Wow, our first avalanche." Was he hoping to experience *more* avalanches?! And my friend Braelynn Gunderson had told me *I* was a little weird. After a moment of taking big breaths, Sawyer stood up straight, and smiled at Marshall and me. His brow abruptly wrinkled and he leaned his head towards mine and carefully pushed my helmet up an inch or so to look at my forehead. "This looks sore, Marlee. Are you okay?"

I had forgotten about my forehead until now. I gently patted the spot with my gloved hand. "I'm not sure, but we need to help Lydie."

"Where *is* Lydie?" he looked around worriedly.

"Lyd's over there, able to breathe, but her leg looks, uh," Marshall looked at his feet, "hurt."

Sawyer looked way more concerned when Marshall mentioned Lydie's undiagnosed injury, so we rushed back to her location. I barely noticed the snow melting off of my helmet and running down my neck. As I worked to help scoop around Lydie's legs, the chilly drops helped cool me as I sweated from the hard work. I was gaining a new appreciation for those construction guys who shoveled cement all last summer in our town. No wonder they were ripped.

When Ellie reached Lydie's cove, she screamed with joy and threw her arms around Lydie's shoulders. "Ellie!" Lydie said,

"I was so worried when you let go of my arm."

Ellie's face wrinkled in grief at the memory. "I held on with all my strength, Lydie. I tried to pull you to the ridge, but you were literally swept away from me." A small sob escaped.

I patted her back and whispered, "You did great to stay with her so long." Ellie nodded and brushed away a tear. Even though Ellie can drive us bonkers, I've never questioned that she completely loves Lydie and me.

Seeing one of us tumble tragically down a mountainside would be as much Ellie's nightmare as ours.

"But look at your leg, Lyd," Ellie cracked and was now all-out crying. I put my arm around her shoulders and held her for a moment while Sawyer and Marshall continued digging around Lydie's legs.

Lydie whimpered in pain, which only made Ellie cry harder seeing that our baby sister was hurting. Marshall and Sawyer exchanged a concerned look with each other before Marshall suggested, "Maybe two of us should go for help. I mean, it looks like Lydie needs a doctor, so maybe we should set out to try to reach the ranger station. A search and rescue team will know how to safely move her."

Everyone stopped and looked at Marshall. While what he said made perfect sense, nobody was thrilled at the idea of splitting up so soon after being reunited. And, as much as I wanted to stay with my sisters, it was plain to see that Sawyer was the leader of our group, and kind of the father figure, so I thought it would be beneficial to keep him and Ellie with Lydie. Also, I was not a fan of the idea of three girls alone in the wilderness. I would feel much better if each group had a guy, for strength and protection. "I'm feeling pretty strong," I started, nodding toward Sawyer's favored leg, "I could hike out with Marshall."

Sawyer nodded thoughtfully before Ellie asked him about his leg. "It hurts, but I think it's very minor compared to Lydie's," he acknowledged. Ellie nodded, concern in her eyes.

"Hey, what about the satellite messenger?" Ellie asked suddenly, reminding us all of our form of emergency communication. Cell phones aren't reliable in the backcountry. Maybe from the peak we could get service, but not below the ridge. So that left the satellite messenger to send out basic messages.

Marshall looked down with a disgusted expression and muttered, "It was in my pack. And my pack is lost in the snow. Along with one of the first aid kits."

"But we still have gorp," I added cheerily, pointing to my pack. Raisins and peanuts can be pretty boring, especially by the third or fourth day of a trek, but hey, food is food.

"And we still have a first aid kit in my pack," Ellie noted.

Sawyer's face as he digested the news that our satellite messenger was gone conveyed feelings of sheer alarm. Not like I wasn't alarmed too, but I tried to swallow my fear again. Tried.

Without saying, we all knew what that meant. The satellite messenger had a button that would immediately alert the local authorities that we needed help and it would provide our exact location. Bringing it along, we had planned that *if* an emergency happened, we could alert rescuers, who would quickly find us and send word to our parents.

And everything would have been just fine. *So now what?*

Ellie quietly checked her phone, but shook her head slowly and resealed the phone in a plastic pouch and zipped it back in her jacket pocket.

Without the satellite messenger, we had no form of communication with anyone besides each other. And God.

"We should pray," I proposed. The group nodded in unison, and I was going to start the prayer, but was suddenly so overcome with emotion that I couldn't speak.

Lydie, who had mostly been silent all along, spoke up and prayed a beautiful, heartfelt prayer. She thanked God for our protection through the avalanche and asked for His divine help out of the situation. She even remembered to ask God to comfort and calm our parents as they woke up to our absence. Lydie's prayer was so passionate that I suddenly realized she was growing into a fine young lady. Little Lydie was no longer a little girl. The realization that my baby sister was maturing into a young woman hit me almost as hard as the avalanche.

At the conclusion of Lydie's prayer, the expressions worn by everyone else revealed that we all must have had the same thought regarding Lydie. She smiled, a bit more energetically this time, and then said, "Well, I'll keep an eye on Ellie and Sawyer while you two go for help."

Ahh, Lydie's comic relief was perfectly timed, and we all let out a nervous laugh.

2

___

Just a few hours ago I had been soundly asleep in my sleeping bag nestled next to Lydie. Since she was the youngest, we put her in the middle, between Ellie and me. Dad and Mom had a tent to themselves. Every summer, our family took a backpacking trip with the Miles family. Dad and Caleb Miles had worked together, guiding backpacking treks before they married our moms. Once their wives and children came along, they found year-round employment elsewhere, but the mountains are still their home-away-from-home – where they come alive.

So, every year, Dad and Caleb plan a weeklong trip for our families together. I must have inherited Dad's love for the peaks, because I find myself longing for the mountain air almost every other day of the year. We live in small-town Wisconsin, and we live a very blessed life. But something about the mountains is invigorating, and we dream of the annual trip all year. We've gone to several places in Colorado, Washington once, and Montana twice. This year we're back in Colorado, where Dad and Caleb joke that they grew up, even though they were both raised in the Midwest.

Three months ago, when Dad announced to us that we were bound for Colorado again, my sisters and I enthusiastically began researching the area. We had briefly read an article about avalanche survival, but who knew we would actually need to know about it.

Right after we read the avalanche survival information, I remember teasing Ellie that Sawyer had probably grown up quite a bit since last year. "What if he's super handsome this summer?" I taunted her.

"That'll be the day," she muttered. "Even *if* his appearance has, um, matured, he's probably the same old annoying Sawyer." She and Sawyer usually spent most of the week together quarrelling about trivial stuff, like whose pack was heavier, who had a better GPA that school year, and even whose hiking boots smelled the least offensive at the end of a day.

I often teased Ellie about Sawyer, mainly because they are only six months apart in age, but also because I really think they would be compatible if they could just decide not to annoy each other. It's like my mom always says, "People will live up or down to the expectations set for them." If Ellie expects Sawyer to be a nuisance, he will seem like a bur in a sock. "Mind over matter," I told her, but she rolled her eyes at me, warning me to drop the discussion. Seriously though, if she expected him to be helpful and intelligent, I really think she would see his positive attributes. To be fair though, Sawyer teases her endlessly, making fun of her perfectionism and the attention she pays to her all-too-beautiful hair. So I can kind of see why she dislikes him. But nothing pushed Ellie over the edge like the day Sawyer called her Smelly.

It was the first summer we went to Montana, and we girls and our moms had a hard time keeping up with Dad and Caleb's fast pace. As we finally approached the campsite, Sawyer and Marshall slowed their pace to hike in with the "estrogen herd" as Sawyer called us. Out of nowhere, a blond-haired grizzly bear sauntered across the trail ahead of us, stopped to look at us, then turned and ran away. The sighting was phenomenal, and I hope to remember it for as long as I live. That bear's muscles rippled under his coat, and he must have weighed 600 pounds. The expression in his eyes was terrifying and humbling and empowering all at once. When he turned to look at us, all seven of us came to a sudden halt and our breaths were caught mid-air. The grizzly stared at us for about four seconds, spun, and ran out of sight.

"Aww, Smelly, you scared him off!" Sawyer joked.

Lydie and I couldn't help but chuckle. Okay, laugh! Mom and Julia even smiled and rolled their eyes when Marshall claimed that he had read that bears are deterred by stinky girls.

Sawyer looked proud of the timing of his joke, at least until Ellie marched up to him and slyly said, "You think you know what smelly is?" She shocked us all when she shoved the bandana that had ridden on her hairline for two full days in his face before jogging ahead to pitch our tent. I thought she was going along with his joke, but she later confided in me that Sawyer's taunt had hurt her feelings. It turns out she had been worried about BO, and when not only her first name, but also her hygiene were made fun of, it gouged her like a knife into warm butter. The rest of the evening, she wouldn't come out of the tent, much less acknowledge Sawyer. Mom and Lydie had a difficult time convincing her to come out to eat. Of course, being in bear country, eating in the tent was not an option since the scent would linger and could attract bears to our tent.

When she finally agreed to come to the cooking site to eat her supper, she held her head down the whole time. Then she insisted on using her deodorant once more before Dad and Caleb hung the bear bag full of "smellables." Sawyer attempted to apologize, but she physically pushed him away. Marshall snickered.

Sometimes I wondered what happened to her beloved lime-green bandana. Well, it started as lime-green, but after three treks and Ellie's three summers at camp, followed by one summer of working as a counselor, the sun had faded the top side to a whitish green.

Even though Ellie and Sawyer have never seen eye to eye, I think of him as the big brother I always dreamed of having. Once, several years ago, I wandered away from camp after supper, and found myself taking a picture of two bear cubs. The cubs were pretty young, I guessed, and Teddy-bear cute. Before I realized there was danger, Sawyer grabbed me by my shoulders and slowly backed me out of the situation. In just a minute, I saw the mother bear and my heart dropped. "Where there are baby bears, you can count on there being a mama bear. And near a mama bear and her cubs is a place you never want to be," Sawyer gently warned. Ever since then, I have used much better bear safety practices, and to be honest, the occurrence also earned Sawyer a ton of trust in my mind.

When Sawyer first suggested the idea of a moonlit summit when we arrived two days ago, I pictured a peaceful, lovely hike, mostly lit by the full moon. The five of us kids casually walked away from the camp to discuss our plan, out of earshot of our parents.

"Full moons come once a month, and this combined-family backpacking trip happens once a year," Sawyer explained. "My plan is for us to make it to the peak by two, maybe three a.m., and then be back to camp well before our parents wake up. They'll never even notice we were gone." He glanced at each of our faces to gauge our reactions. My mind began spinning, imagining the cautionary information Dad and Caleb would have for this idea.

Hiking at night? Attempting a peak in the dark? It was early June, so the ridges and peaks were still mostly snow-covered. During the day, with Dad and Caleb's expertise, our careful moms close by, and the extensive gear that our dads had, I would not be so hesitant. But sneaking away in the night, just us kids? I almost spoke up, but then Sawyer continued, "I heard Dad and Mr. Forrest talk about it once." Forrest Stanley is my dad, affectionately called Mr. Forrest by the Miles boys. Sawyer continued, "They did a moonlit summit, and Dad said it was one of his greatest memories. We could have a story like that, too," he pressed. I too had heard the story of their midnight hike. But they told the guys they were with what they were doing, and besides, they were professional backpacking guides at the time.

In my family, we pray to God. A lot. We pray before meals and trips, and at the start and end of every day. Instinctively, I began praying silently, either for safety or for Sawyer to forget this whole idea. I'll admit, it sounded cool – make that awesome. Summiting one of Colorado's fourteeners, a peak over 14,000 feet tall, in the middle of the night during a full moon! What could be better than that? This would be a tough decision. Sawyer was almost eighteen now, with a respectable amount of backpacking experience considering his age. He was enrolled to attend the Professional Outdoor Guides School at the end of summer. So we practically had a pro leading us. Well, not quite a pro, but I knew he was good for his age.

And I already knew how knowledgeable he was with bears. I'd seen him hike every summer for as long as I could remember, and I could not deny that he was a natural. With him as our guide, the chances of our succeeding were fairly high – I hoped.

And I could see his reasoning for not telling our parents. I mean, what kind of parents would agree to let their children attempt such a hike? Certainly not ours. Yet, even in our youth, the five of us were probably more prepared for a midnight hike than the average American adult. As long as we didn't ask our parents, we would not be disobeying, right? Careless perhaps, but not disobedient. At least, I hoped not.

"No way," voiced Ellie. Normally I would have given her opinion equal consideration, but since she was talking to Sawyer, I dismissed her negative response as simply wanting to disagree with Sawyer.

Sawyer shot her a challenging look and without missing a beat, roughly asked, "Why? Ellie, what about this is a bad idea?"

Ellie's eyes grew huge and her face had an expression that said, "Are you out of your mind?"

"One," Ellie held up a finger, "it's night. Hiking where

you can't see is 100 percent dangerous. *Maybe* if we were familiar with the trail, but we're not. Two," she popped up her second finger, "we're not going to tell anyone our plan? Hello, Sawyer Miles, did you totally forget the first cardinal rule of mountaineering? Three," up shot her third finger, "you would be insane to drag little Lydie into the wilderness. She is *eleven*, for crying out loud!" (As if Lydie wasn't already in the wilderness, but whatever.)

I had to agree with two of Ellie's points, and from Sawyer's face, he was either hurt by Ellie's speech or he was considering her points, probably already planning his counter. Before anyone had a chance to say anything though, Lydie argued, "*Little* Lydie? Come on, Sis, I always get left out. I'm sick of being excluded from all the fun stuff. When you were eleven, you got to go on that rock climbing trip with the church kids, and when Marlee was eleven, she went to camp *for a week* in California with the Gundersons. *Come on,* Ellie! We'll be with Sawyer and Marshall, and we'll only be out for *one night*." Lydie wore a confident, slightly proud expression as she looked at Ellie, and realized she too had made a good point. Or was that two points? My mind was spinning.

Sawyer gloated, but rather than keeping quiet, he shot up one finger just inches from Ellie's eyes and said, "One, we'll have our headlamps. And the full moon. And spare batteries for our headlamps. Two," up went another finger, "we'll bring Dad's satellite GPS messenger along. Three," his third finger nearly hit Ellie's nose as she glared at him, "Lydie is strong for her size and conditioned for hiking." With that, Sawyer focused a daring stare into Ellie's eyes. My teasing Ellie about the possibility of Sawyer having grown up this last year was not in vain. Seeing him stare down at my older sister, I estimated him to be at least six feet tall, several inches taller than at last year's trip. His shoulders were broader too, and he looked like he probably worked out hard and often, probably to maintain good condition for these very hiking trips.

I half expected Ellie to retort back, or to shove Sawyer and storm off, but with a somewhat defeated countenance, she glanced at Marshall, "Marsh, what are your thoughts?"

Marshall lit up, "I'm going with my bro, whether or not you girls decide to join us," he confidently stated.

That did it. We were in. I cast an inquisitive look at Marshall, wondering if he had planned his last statement, knowing that a challenge like referring to us as "you girls" would influence Ellie to agree. Marshall was fifteen, like me, but he was usually quiet enough that I couldn't describe his personality very well. Honestly, I don't know Marshall as well as I know Sawyer, which is why I wasn't sure if he purposely worded his decision as a challenge to convince us to come. Not that Lydie needed any convincing. Or that I needed *much* convincing. And while Ellie did put up a valiant stand against Sawyer, I think she secretly was intrigued by the thought of the moonlit hike. I was positive that the only reason she fought the idea was because Sawyer was the one who suggested it. Well, that and the risks involved.

Ellie isn't always disagreeable. In fact, she is usually very amiable. Granted, maybe due to her being firstborn, she is strong-willed and tends to strive for perfection. My mom constantly tells her that only God can be perfect, and we should be content with doing our personal best, but that is not good enough for Ellie. She will push herself as close to perfection as is humanly possible. Once, her county fair project on floral arrangements earned a second place ribbon, and she argued with the judges and even went so far as to research why her arrangement should earn a blue ribbon, if not a purple-champion ribbon. The judges finally gave her a blue ribbon, but I always wondered if it was because they were sick and tired of her explanations rather than that they agreed with Ellie. She was smug that day, but this was different. I could see she felt defeated that Sawyer had won the debate.

And so, the five of us quietly prepared for our trek. Lydie was so eager that her hands were literally shaking and her smile was mischievous and wide. Marshall looked just as excited, which says a lot. He's usually reserved and hard to read. Looking at Lydie, I was beginning to feel the thrill, though my heart raced with questions and prayers pleading for safety. When I glanced to observe Ellie's face, I noticed that her eyes were fixed on Sawyer's face. At first I thought she was glaring at him, but her face didn't look angry. It seemed like she looked at him with a look of admiration, if that was possible – almost as if she did trust him and sincerely wanted to go on this midnight hike after all. Maybe she was just a bit apprehensive, like me. But when I turned my focus back to Sawyer as he rattled off our itinerary, I noticed that he was focused on Ellie's face. And for once, he didn't appear to be exasperating her. Maybe my teasing wasn't far-fetched, I mused with a sudden smile. *Sawyer and Ellie...*

"What?" asked Sawyer, turning to me.

Startled, I repeated his, "What?"

"Why are you smiling like that? It looks like you're planning something evil," he suspiciously said.

"And you're not?" My retort was all I could think of in the moment.

He sheepishly smiled, and I again saw Ellie look at him warmly. Weird!

"Back to business! Here are your individual packing lists," Sawyer said as Marshall began passing out small sheets of paper. "Lydie takes the smallest load of course. I'll take the biggest."

"You made us individual packing lists?" Ellie asked with complete disgust in her voice. The warm look I thought she had given Sawyer had been replaced with absolute irritation, as if he were a skunk who had just sprayed. "I mean," her voice softened, realizing the brashness in her response, "it's good that you planned ahead, but, I mean, seriously, *you think we need you* to tell us what to pack for a peak?"

Yikes, that one hurt! I could tell immediately from Sawyer's dejected look that Ellie had hurt his ego. While I didn't think it necessary to tell us what to pack, I certainly wasn't offended that our self-appointed guide had taken the time to consider the appropriate gear and how best to distribute it. Honestly, I thought it was a good indicator that we had a trustworthy guide. Obviously, Sawyer hadn't dreamt this up on a whim. And, since he'd be attending POGS this fall, he was obviously pursuing a mountaineering profession like his father had. Likely he viewed this as the perfect opportunity to practice for his future career. I thought about speaking up to say that I trusted Sawyer or to thank him for the packing list, but decided against it as I didn't want to create any fissures between Ellie and me.

"Wow, thanks Sawyer!" Leave it to Lydie to break the tension. "I can't wait! I'll go pack right now!" And with that, she gave Sawyer the kind of hug that a kid would give her uncle, then raced back to our tent. Sawyer appeared to appreciate Lydie's kindness, but I noticed that he would not even glance at Ellie. Ellie, however, was either being stubborn or was completely unaware that her words had stung. After a moment of studying her list, she marched back to our tent.

Skimming my packing list, I saw a problem. Crampons were on my list, except I didn't have my own pair yet. Dad said I wasn't experienced enough for crampons, and with my level of skill, crampons would serve more as a danger than an aid. Crampons strap onto the bottom of hiking boots and they help mountaineers gain traction in snow and ice. Made of metal, their sharp blades can cause serious injury to an inexperienced user, or even to an experienced climber in a fall.

"Hey, Sawyer," he looked my way and from the corner of my eye, I saw Marshall look at me too, and I was afraid they expected me to act rudely like my older sister. "Um, I see I should pack crampons. I've been asking Dad for two years now, but he keeps saying I'm not ready for a pair. So, um," I looked down, thinking that Marshall had probably had a pair of crampons for two or three seasons, "I don't have any," I muttered, feeling embarrassed.

He thought for a moment, and then said, "Tell you what, if we get to a spot where we need crampons, we'll rope up. If your dad isn't comfortable giving you crampons yet, I certainly shouldn't overrule that. But if we're all roped up, and Marshall, Ellie and I have crampons, we should be good." I was impressed with his problem solving and his respect for my dad and politeness to me in this embarrassing situation, and it further increased my trust in his plan. Smiling, I thanked him and then apologized for Ellie's impolite treatment. When I mentioned her name, he looked in the direction of our tent and seemed to grow uncomfortable.

"I just thought," he began quietly, "well, I thought that if I could plan a successful trip, it might prove to Ellie that I'm not still the annoying twerp she despises." I noticed his neck grow red as he finished his explanation, and I also saw Marshall give his brother a knowing look. Was Sawyer saying that he liked my sister? Or maybe he was just hoping to make up for the Smelly incident. Why else would he need to prove to Ellie that he was capable of planning a hike? We already knew that he had planned several short trips for his local backpacking club, so surely he didn't need to prove himself to his family. He wanted to impress Ellie! I wasn't sure if that was possible, but hey, I could root for him.

Back to the obvious safety issue, I could understand why he opted to keep our adventure a secret, but I still wasn't sold on the part about not telling *anyone* our whereabouts. I almost asked if we could alert the local ranger, but I knew that the ranger would insist on telling our parents, which would certainly put a stop to the plan. Besides, the idea of seeing the world from this peak during a full moon was starting to thrill me.

And, I couldn't ignore the fact that the full moon happened to land on the night two full days before our families were scheduled to summit according to Dad and Caleb's plan, which would give us adequate recovery time. Maybe this trip was meant to be after all. Feeling a new wave of assurance, I headed toward the tent to pack.

"Supper's ready!" Mom and Julia Miles called. Dad and Caleb had gone to the stream and pumped our water. Usually we would have all gone to purify our own drinking water, but I just now realized that we kids had been so caught up in our plans that we completely missed their short trip to the stream. I hoped that during supper our parents wouldn't ask what we had talked about.

As the nine of us gathered around two small backpacking stoves, Caleb said the prayer. I noticed that he asked God to bless our families not only with safety and fun, but also with a new sense of unity. Unity – that made me think. I remembered Dad and Mom saying how backpacking often brings groups together like no other experience. Struggling through the wilderness together, offering first aid to each other, spending every waking minute with a group, enjoying the happy moments of victory and enduring the tiring moments of blisters and lost trails could unite a group of individuals into a tight-knit family. Maybe this teenagers-plus-Lydie midnight hike would be just the thing to unify us.

I even convinced myself that Caleb's prayer gave us the go-ahead to take this hike. Okay, now, I was fully ready for this. Mentally, anyway.

3

———

I woke hearing a muffled cough just outside our girls' tent. That was the plan. Not wanting to attract any attention to our departure, Sawyer drank two whole liters of water just before bed. Two liters sounds excessive, but after a day on the trails, nothing tastes better than cold, mountain stream water. And this early in June, the streams are filled with snow melt from higher in the mountains, so the water is so crisp and cool that it is easy to guzzle a liter.

When Sawyer woke up to relieve himself, Marshall tiptoed to our tent and coughed a few times before tapping the sides of our tent to wake us. I wasn't sure that coughing in the night would wake me up, not during a backpacking trek. Usually while on trail, I could sleep through a tornado. The fresh air, combined with hiking all day long while carrying a 25 pound backpack puts me into a deep, long sleep. I suppose the anticipation for what was ahead of us caused an adrenaline surge when I heard his cough.

Lydie was the first to pop up, and pop she did, reminding me of a popcorn kernel. Eyes bright, she eagerly began shaking Ellie. Typically Lydie is slow to wake, spending three to four minutes rubbing her eyes and rolling back and forth, as if she could somehow roll time back to nighttime. Then after a few enormous yawns, she stretches her arms and finally sits up, opening her eyes. I've shared a room with Lydie since she was little, so I'm as familiar with her sleeping patterns as I am with my own.

Meanwhile I sat up and stretched my arms toward the top of the tent, feeling the excitement wipe away my grogginess. While on trail, our families usually turn in for the night about 8:00 p.m. It sounds early, but after a full day of hiking, tired feet and bodies crave a comfy sleeping bag. And in the mountains, the sun sets much earlier than it does in a non-mountainous area, due to the height of the peaks blocking the sun's rays. Once the sun sets, the temperature drops quickly, and burrowing into a down-filled sleeping bag feels like a cold washcloth on a feverish forehead. Rising at 11:45 p.m., my mind and body were not ready to start another day, but my adrenaline was.

Ellie's sour attitude had been overtaken by positive

energy. Apparently, she had applied my "mind over matter" speech. The thought made me giggle, thinking that something I had said would have inspired my older sister. Truth be told, she probably reached this attitude by her own determination.

We had agreed that not a word would be spoken until we were across the meadow from where we camped, just to ensure our quiet departure. Silently, we reached for our headlamps, mindlessly laced our boots, loaded our relatively small packs onto our backs, and began the walk to meet the boys at the other side of the grassy plain. When we met the boys, their faces glowed in the moonlight and they looked as bright eyed as if it were noon.

"Morning, girls," Sawyer nodded. Marshall just grinned.

"First things first, we pray," Sawyer stated. Everyone bowed their heads, and I linked arms with my sisters. Sawyer began, "Dear Father in heaven, You are amazing. We see this wilderness You have created, and we are humbled." Wow, Sawyer had grown up. I didn't dare sneak a peek at Ellie right now. "We are stoked to have this opportunity to take this moonlit hike. I pray that You would keep each of us under the shadow of Your wings and return us to our parents safe and sound. And thank You again for this trek. In Jesus' name, Amen."

We all quietly nodded, "Amen," and then, without

ng my head, I glanced at Ellie. She was giving Sawyer that same warm, respectful look that I had seen just before the packing list incident. Sawyer did not notice as he turned to lead the way.

For the first hour, we hiked without talking much. Our boots crunched on the rocks, which gradually became covered in snow as we gained elevation. As we walked on in single file, led by Sawyer, then Marshall, Lydie, me, and Ellie in the rear, we watched the moon climb higher into the night sky. We heard an owl, watched a porcupine cross the trail just ahead of us, and startled a coyote away from his catch. Most of the time, we did not even need our headlamps. A few times in the trees, we clicked them on, but when we reached tree line, it may as well have been 10:00 a.m., as bright as the moon shone.

The night temperature was cool and comfortable for hiking. I felt almost like I was dreaming, with the beautiful moon overhead lighting our way and the sounds of nature accompanying our hike. It was beautiful, and I found myself thanking God for, as Sawyer had prayed, this wonderful opportunity. I hoped that I would remember the hike forever.

As the grade steepened into the ridge, we stepped away from the last of the trees. We were at tree line, where trees no longer grow on a mountain. Sawyer stopped and motioned for us to gather around. Huddled in a circle, I could see that Sawyer was pleased to see four smiles beaming at him.

"All right Ellie, don't thank me yet, but go ahead and tell me I was right this time," Sawyer said lightheartedly.

I watched Ellie carefully, and to my surprise, she did not look annoyed at Sawyer. Instead, she playfully rolled her eyes and her lower jaw moved sideways before she admitted, "Yes, Sawyer Miles. You were right. This hike is," she paused as if looking for an adjective that could possibly sum up this experience, "extraordinary," she finished.

Though we all agreed with her word choice, nobody could believe that she had commended Sawyer. I actually saw Sawyer's jaw drop before he smiled at Ellie. Before her compliment could go to his head though, she playfully punched his shoulder and said, "Where next, Captain?"

Lydie, Marshall, Sawyer, and I turned to stare at Ellie.

Never before had Ellie said anything so supportive to Sawyer. Maybe she was the one who had grown up more. Calling him Captain was instilling in him that he was worthy of our trust, that he had authority. I expected Ellie to have fought for the leadership role of this hike, but when she asked him where the trail went next, and then called him Captain, I realized that Ellie was letting him lead. Wow. I could only imagine the satisfaction that Sawyer must have felt. Then I snuck a look at his face and could see the satisfaction visibly written in his eyes and smile. And even in the moonlight, I think his cheeks grew red. Quite red as he continued to smile at Ellie. At that moment, she evidently felt embarrassed by what she had said, and she quickly turned away from the group and made a big deal out of checking the time on her wristwatch.

"Next, we hike up the ridge," Sawyer explained and pointed with his hand. "I can see from here that it's pretty snow-packed in a couple hundred yards, so Ellie and Marshall, be ready to put on your crampons. When we break to put them on, we'll rope up, with Lydie and Marlee sandwiched between climbers wearing crampons. Let's put Lydie in the center position since she's the only climber without an ice axe." Lydie nodded in agreement. I was confident with Sawyer's plan. Being roped up would keep the group together in the event that one of us would lose footing. If that happened, the falling climber would shout, "Falling!" and all the other climbers would "self arrest" with their ice axes. To self-arrest means to throw your body against the ground, forcing the ice axe into the snow, which makes an anchor. Hopefully the anchoring system created by digging four ice axes into the snow would stop the fall before the climber slid too far. It made perfect sense to arrange us so that Lydie and I were surrounded by climbers with crampons.

I reached my hand to the base of my pack and lightly

felt my ice axe. Dad had practiced with me at least a dozen times this past winter at a park near our home. Up the steep bank we'd walk, and then without warning he would push me into the hill. I had to shout, "Falling!" and practice my self-arrest technique, where I held the T-shaped head of the ice axe against my chest, rolled onto my stomach, and firmly pushed the pick end into the snow. The goal is to stop quickly, because of course, the longer the slide, the faster you fall, which becomes very dangerous in rocky environments. Dad and I practiced long enough that I felt mostly sure of my ability to react properly. I was glad to have the chance to use my ice axe for real, in the mountains of Colorado.

Just as Sawyer said, a couple of hundred yards up the ridge the snow began to feel slick. Our boots sank in almost to our knees, and he halted us and began skillfully tying bowline knots in his climbing rope. Looking at his rope, I could tell that it was new, and I was sure that Sawyer was ecstatic to be breaking it in with a moonlit summit.

"Is that the peak?" Lydie interrupted my quiet inspection of the rope.

"Afraid it's a false summit, Lydie," Sawyer said. "According to my guide book, we'll climb over two false summits before finally seeing the top of this mountain."

"How are we doing on time?" Marshall asked as he curled down to fasten his crampons onto his boots.

"We made excellent time this far, which is good, because with this grade and now the snow, we'll slow down quite a bit. We'll have less dense oxygen at this elevation, even compared to last night's camp. The plan is to either peak or turn back no later than 3:00, so we can be sure to be back by the time our parents wake up at 6:00," Sawyer explained.

Sawyer tied each of our waists into loops on his rope, with Marshall closely observing his every move. I noticed Sawyer dramatically slow down his tying of two of the knots so his brother could better see how to form the bowline on a bight. A bight is a loop of rope. Watching him expertly tie us in and kindly show his brother proved to me that he would make a fantastic guide. Ellie must have had a similar thought, because I saw her shyly watch Sawyer as he tied her knot. When he finished it and looked up, she gave him a timid smile, which he returned.

"Helmets on and buckled," he announced, quickly snapping back to the task at hand.

"Ready," four voices called back.

Up we went. We must have climbed up the ridge twenty minutes at a steady pace when suddenly the snow disappeared. "How does this happen?" I asked to anyone who had an answer. As elevation increases, air's ability to hold moisture and heat decrease, meaning that the higher the mountain, the more snow there usually is.

"I suppose," Sawyer began thoughtfully, "that this ridge had just enough sunlight in the last two weeks to melt the snow up here. But since it's still early in summer, the sun is not high enough to dry up the snow lower on the mountain. And considering the steep grade, the snow up here probably slid down the mountain, explaining the knee deep snow we just encountered. Regardless of the reason, we need to take off our crampons. And I guess we can untie. It looks dry the whole way to the next false peak."

In just minutes we were untied and hiking up again, our pace increasing now that the rocks were dry. The ridge to the next false peak, a high point in a mountain that appears to be the summit from certain angles, was a relatively easy climb, and we made it quickly. As we surfaced the top of the false peak, our heads instinctively tilted up and we gazed at the next highest point, which, according to Sawyer's guide book, was the real peak. Well over fourteen thousand feet above sea level, it was an enormous beauty. And there we stood, with just another hour of hiking between us and what seemed to be the top of the world. We all gazed at that summit, and then exchanged eager smiles with one another. Lydie looked ready to bubble over with joy. Marshall and I seemed to share the same sentiment of wonder, while Ellie looked genuinely radiant in the moonlight. Sawyer reminded me of a proud father, ready to congratulate his family for an impressive accomplishment. In a way, he was. This hike had been his idea, so watching us approach the top of the mountain must have thrilled him.

The mountain face that loomed ahead of us was covered in snow. It angled toward the south, and it sure was a beauty in the bright moonlight. At first I found it odd that this side was again covered in snow, considering how dry the last false peak we climbed was, but then I remembered Dad explaining to me that south-facing slopes often have lots of wet, heavy snow in spring and summer. And I guessed that this ridge protected the previous false peak from snowstorms. And more than likely there had been an avalanche on the previous slope earlier this season. Up here, the ridge wasn't as steep, so the snow had built up all winter and spring.

With a "Let's do this!" from Marshall, we headed upward. I was about sixteen steps into the snow when I heard the roar. Before my mind even had to time register the cause of the sound, I cried out in panic. Sawyer shouted to us to run to the side of ridge, to try to escape the path of the white monster racing toward us. Where was Lydie? What would happen to my dear baby sister? In an instant, a blur of white, I was highly aware of Sawyer and Ellie racing to get to Lydie. I heard Marshall tell me to swim to stay on top of the snow. When the mass swept under my body, I gasped in horror as I felt the powerful force of nature. The fact that snow in an avalanche settles as densely as cement terrified me as I desperately thrashed my arms and legs and gulped air before crashing down, down into darkness.

The next 20 minutes felt like watching a too-realistic movie. I was terrified, and wished it was just a scary movie that I could turn off and forget. Forget the midnight hike, forget being body-slammed by a wall of snow, forget struggling for air. Then I thought of my parents and my sisters, and I decided to use every ounce of strength to see them again. Hearing Marshall's voice gave me even more reason to fight for life, and when we were all reunited, I felt like we were going to be okay. We had survived an avalanche. Surely we could hike to safety.

4

———

There we were, preparing to split up and find help. Sawyer earnestly talked us through the route on his topographic map, placed it in Marshall's hand with a compass, and after a quick refresher course in orienteering, told us we would probably not get lost since the trail was well-marked. Thanks. I hugged my sisters, waved at Sawyer, and Marshall and I set off. Marshall's watch told us that it was already 8:00 a.m., and I shuddered to think of our parents' distress. Had they gone looking for us? Perhaps they were on their way to the ranger station now. When they noticed that Caleb's satellite messenger was gone, they would likely send out a group to find us. They would freak out when they saw it was lost in the avalanche. They'd follow the GPS coordinates of our messenger to the snowy aftermath of the avalanche and think the worst.

"You know, Marsh," I started, "it was probably extra good that we left the others back on the ridge in case the rescuers track down our location from the satellite messenger."

He nodded and for the first time, looked a bit reassured. As we made our way down the mountain, the snow changed into big boulder-sized chunks of snow. Up where Lydie and I landed the snow was packed tight and fairly level, but down here it almost looked like large rocks coated with snow. We hiked past several broken trees that looked as if they had been dragged a long ways down the mountain. "Maybe we'll find your pack in this mess," I said, but Marshall just shrugged and kept walking. I guess he was really beating himself up for losing his pack.

Then it occurred to me that I still did not know what his avalanche experience was. Although he was rarely in a talkative mood, I was curious, and I thought the conversation would help pass the time as we walked in the direction of the ranger station, which was at least five miles away. Five miles on the side of a mountain. On a long walk such as the one ahead of us, I would appreciate some chatter.

"Were you buried?" I asked. In response, Marshall stopped walking and looked squarely at me. "I mean, in the avalanche," I added. "Did you dig yourself out or did you manage to escape the rush?"

He took a long, slow breath and then began, "Remember when I yelled at you to try to swim and stay on top of the surface?" I nodded. He continued, "Well, just before I said that, I looked up and saw the avalanche." He stopped and the grim look on his face almost made me regret asking, but after a minute he went on, "Marlee, it was the biggest, fiercest act of nature I've ever seen. It was roaring down the mountain at us, and I thought we were all done for." He looked down and slowly shook his head. "I honestly didn't think I had any chance with a pack on my back, so I unbuckled it, shouted to you to swim, and started swimming myself. Miraculously I managed to stay close to the surface, but Marlee, I purposely let my pack go!" he exclaimed in self-disgust.

"Marshall, you did the right thing. Survival, Man! Your life is worth more than any pack!"

"But you all made it out with your packs on. And my pack had our emergency communication!"

"Marsh, who knows, maybe if you had worn your pack, you would have gotten snagged up by one of those trees we saw all busted up toward the bottom. Or maybe, had you worn your pack, you would have gotten stuck in the bottom of the snow and never climbed out! Please don't beat yourself up over this. We'll work through this together."

He lifted his eyes, smiled his appreciation and quietly said, "Thanks, Marlee. I needed to hear that." I smiled, glad that I had been able to encourage him – at least for now. We didn't have time to hold a pity party.

"So, we keep going down?" I asked.

"Until we get to the end of the avalanche, where it runs out between those trees," he pointed. "Then we should turn toward the west and keep just below the ridge at tree line until we hit the trail. Hopefully we can find the trail, and then a few miles on it and we should reach the ranger station. Assuming the ranger is at the station, he or she can call for help and hopefully send word to our parents."

Our parents! I could not imagine how much trouble we would be in for this. Even though I did not want to think about it, I knew we deserved it. Sneaking off in the middle of the night to climb a peak this early in the summer when snow was still melting? We probably had a long lecture ahead of us when we joined up with them.

Climbing down is usually harder on a climber's knees than climbing up, and this became especially true in the rubble of snow boulders. Keeping up with Marshall's pace was strenuous, and I was nearly panting for air. Then I noticed my stomach growl, and remembered that none of us had had anything more than a handful of gorp since last night's supper. I knew that between the five packs, we had enough gorp and granola bars to last a day, and thankfully Sawyer had packed one meal for us all. Good thing that one meal was in his pack. Before Marshall and I set out, we decided to wait to eat, just in case our ordeal became further extended.

As the terrain changed and we walked along tree line, the footing grew easier as we left the path of the avalanche. At least the hike had eased up in difficulty, but I needed a drink of water, so I called ahead to Marshall to ask him to stop for a moment. He looked annoyed and checked his watch, then checked the sky, and then squinted into the distance as he scanned for the trail. As I indulged in the icy water from my bottle, I noticed his brow wrinkle in concern. "Everything okay?" I cautiously asked as I quickly slathered a glop of sunscreen on my face. Sunburn is a big concern in the mountains since there is less atmosphere between climbers and the sun. I knew enough to take the precaution. Fried skin would not help our situation.

"We just need to hurry if we're going to make it to help today. If we're not there by 2:00, I think we'll need to turn back and return to the girls and Sawyer."

I nodded slowly, thinking about his proposition. He was right that we did not have the gear to camp out, so we would need to return to the group before nightfall. I had not even considered that we might not make it to the ranger station today, but as I looked over his shoulder at the map, I realized that it was quite possible we would not make it. Mountain miles take much longer than smooth-sidewalk-in-town-miles. Five miles could easily take most of the day, especially when we had so little food to energize our bodies. I grabbed a handful of raisins and peanuts for myself, passed another handful to Marshall, and then said, "Onward." Marshall nodded silently, took another look at his watch, and resumed hiking, still looking concerned.

Marshall silently pointed out a rock cairn, which is a small heap of rocks that people have constructed to mark the trail. We headed toward it, assuming it marked the trail we needed to take.

After another twenty minutes, Marshall held up his hand and stopped. Not sure why we were stopping, I sent a questioning look his way. He shook his head and said, "The Worst Chivalry Award goes to me." I shrugged my shoulders, not understanding what he said.

"You know, chivalry, it's like manners, how a guy treats a lady," he explained. I nodded slowly, still not sure where he was going with this conversation. "Let me carry your pack," he clarified.

"Oh! I see. Yeah, that would be great if you would, Marshall. I'd appreciate the break. Then maybe I'll be able to keep up with you," I added. I happily shrugged the pack off my back. Even though it probably only weighed fifteen pounds since we had packed just enough for our night hike, I felt very relieved when Marshall lifted it out of my hands. "Thanks."

Marshall mumbled, "I just feel bad that it took me this long to offer."

"I probably would not have let you carry it earlier anyway," I said. It was true. While I appreciated Marshall's *chivalry*, I also felt a need to prove myself and to not appear weak.

Just then we spotted a game trail stemming off toward the south. Ironically, the game trail looked easier to follow than the common trail we were on, and I almost thought it was the hiking trail. I stopped, remembering Sawyer telling us the trail was well-marked so we probably wouldn't get lost, and recalling a dozen times when I looked to Dad who seemed to know instinctively which trail to take. Marshall surveyed our surroundings and after a long, quiet moment, he motioned to an almost hidden branch on the side of "the" trail that clearly had a sawn edge. "Trail clearers last summer sawed that fallen branch," he showed me. Then I saw the other end across the trail, also with a sawn edge. Phew. We weren't lost. Yet.

"What are you daydreaming of eating?" Marshall broke my train of thoughts.

"Hmm?" It took me a moment to think. "Oh, cheese pizza sounds good."

"Cheese pizza? Of all the millions of options for pizza toppings, you'd pick cheese?" Marshall challenged.

"What would you pick? What are you daydreaming of eating?" I prodded.

"I am daydreaming about eating two big beef enchiladas smothered in cheese and hot sauce. And for pizza, I would pick taco pizza any day, any time," he declared.

My eyes widened. "Wow. Is the snow making you daydream about Mexico?"

"Nah," Marshall casually explained, "but I love Mexican food. Any day. Any time."

I laughed. The conversation definitely helped to pass the time. Speaking of food, I noticed that the sun was nearly directly above us, indicating that it was very close to noon. But my stomach had already told me that. My stomach, and a nagging headache that had been taunting me for the past mile or so. "Marshall," I began, but stopped for fear of being a hindrance.

"Yeah?" he asked politely.

"Uh, I," I planned to ask him if he had any pain reliever for my headache, but I suddenly felt very weak.

"Marlee, are you okay?" Marshall stepped toward me and put a supportive hand on my back, almost as if he expected me to collapse.

"I think so. I mean," *yikes, this hunger and headache are making me weak,* I thought, and then tried again to ask for help, "Do we have any headache medicine? I just feel really weak all of a sudden," I admitted.

Marshall quietly groaned to himself, no doubt thinking of the time. I hated to be a bother, but I knew that if I didn't take care of myself, we would have two people to evacuate, which would be more than a bother. Marshall thought for a moment and then quickly looked at my forehead. "We forgot to take care of your cut," he murmured.

I nodded, "Honestly though, I think this headache is due to hunger and stress more than the cut."

"But what if you have a concussion?" he wondered aloud. I did not know what to say to that. I probably would remember a hit strong enough to cause a concussion, but then again, I was unaware that my forehead was cut until Marshall first commented. I'd never had a concussion before and didn't know what it felt like.

Dealing with the issue at hand, Marshall took charge and had me sit in the snow. "Start sipping water," he handed me one of my bottles out of my pack before reaching for our gorp, "and eat a couple handfuls of this." Thankfully we had divvied up our remaining first aid kit from Ellie's pack before splitting up, and Marshall quickly located a mild pain reliever, carefully measured the appropriate dose, and watched me closely as I swallowed the medicine with some more fresh water. "You're not doing too well are you?" Marshall gently asked. Normally I would have been offended at the negative comment, but there was no use in pretending this time.

I lowered my head. "I thought I was doing better than I am now," referring to when we first decided to split up.

"Sawyer was limping pretty badly and I thought I was in better shape than him. And I thought that Lydie should have her oldest sister to comfort her."

Marshall nodded, no longer looking annoyed. He checked his watch again. "Well, it's 1:30. According to the map, we're still at least a four hours' hike from the ranger station. Let's break a little longer to perk us both up, and then we'll head back to the avalanche."

I nodded, but was biting back tears. We had set out to find help, and all we accomplished was tiring ourselves. Lydie was in pain, everyone was hungry, and without a tent and sleeping bags, we were going to be dangerously cold tonight. Marshall noticed my somber face and kindly said, "Marlee, it's not your fault. We're all working on just a few hours of sleep and only snacks and water."

"But what about tonight? How will we keep warm?" Although Marshall and I were comfortable in short-sleeved shirts now, hiking low on the mountain, we knew full well that at night, especially above tree line, the temperature would be frigid.

Marshall remained calm and matter-of-factly answered, "We'll all just huddle together with Lydie in the middle, and Sawyer and me on the edges. Maybe Sawyer and Ellie even made a wind block today with snow," he added hopefully. "We'll hike back to them, make a nice warm meal, and huddle up for the night."

I was glad Marshall sounded so confident, and I

wondered if he really felt that confident or if he was forcing himself to stay calm, much like I had done right after he rescued me from the avalanche. *Somebody needs to stay calm,* I thought as we turned and began hiking away from the ranger station, away from any progress we had made. My thoughts drifted to Lydie, Ellie and Sawyer, and I wondered who the one remaining calm in that group was.

Marshall must have been wondering the exact same question, because he suddenly said, "Who do you suppose is the calm one back in the snow?" And then he smiled mischievously, "I wonder if Sawyer and Ellie are cooperating today?"

Marshall laughed when I told him that our trains of thought were on the same track. "I can hardly believe how well those two are getting along this summer," I quickly said. Such a drastic change was hard to ignore.

Marshall agreed, "It sure is a difference compared to the last eight years backpacking together. I just worry that at any moment Ellie will snap when it dawns on her that we're in this predicament because of Sawyer's idea for the moonlit peak hike. I don't even want to think about what she'd say, or yell, at my brother."

Marshall had a good point. Without Sawyer's challenge for this hike, we'd probably be with our parents, safe and sound. Yet, we had all agreed to go along with Sawyer's plan. But something about what

Marshall said, that he didn't want to think about what Ellie would yell at Sawyer, had me curious.

"You mean, guys care what girls say to, or yell at, them?" I suddenly asked.

Marshall looked at me, "Well, yeah," he said, as if the fact was the most obvious truth in the world. "Marlee, guys practically live to impress girls. When a girl says something mean to us or about us, it hurts. I mean, if another guy says something mean, whether or not it's true, it might make me mad, but I'll get over it pretty soon. But when a girl talks bad about a guy," he shook his head, "that does damage. Serious damage. What a girl says can pretty much make or break a guy."

I was amazed to learn all of this. Having two sisters, I did not have much understanding about guys. While I knew boys, I had never thought of them as, I don't know, vulnerable. They always seem so tough and thick-skinned. Even arrogant a lot of the time. "Has Ellie said something that hurt Sawyer before?" I asked, immediately thinking of her rude comments when Sawyer first introduced his midnight hike plan.

Marshall's look told me that our trains of thought were again on the exact same track.

"Have I ever said something that hurt like that?" I grew worried about what I may have unknowingly said.

Marshall shook his head, "Nah, you're like the mediator of your bunch. You're usually nice and encouraging." I was glad for his answer, and very glad for his disclosure, because now I would sure try to avoid being hurtful.

"How's your headache?"

"Talking helps," I said.

Marshall threw his head back and laughed, "Only a girl would get headache relief from talking!"

I playfully punched him on the arm and then quickly said, "Oh, no! Was that hurtful?"

Marshall theatrically clutched his arm and curled down to his knees with a mock groan.

"You know what I meant," I defended.

Marshall nodded. "I've never been physically beaten up by a girl before. Just keep in mind that girls have the ability to verbally beat us up. But, like I said before, you're pretty good about being decent with what you say. Just, you know, keep it in mind. For future reference. And don't hesitate to share it with Ellie," he concluded with a slight smile.

I smiled. "Thank you, Marshall."

"Yeah, yeah, that's enough talking for me. Your turn," he said good-naturedly.

5

___

When Marshall and I eventually slugged back to the base of the avalanche, he let out a long, low whistle. "Wow! That snowmass did more damage in one minute than a bulldozer could have done in a whole day," he observed.

I simply nodded. I had to agree that the aftermath was nearly as frightening as the actual avalanche. Right now, though, I was so tired and hungry that I did not have enough energy to talk. We quickly spotted our group toward the ridge, probably another thousand feet ahead of us. Marshall largely waved his arms, but if they saw us, they did not wave back. I could see that they had lit a fire, probably in hopes of alerting anyone in search for us of our location. Though the smoke did not stand out like black on white, a search team would surely keep their eyes peeled for the slightest sign of our whereabouts.

Oddly, knowing that we were this close zapped me of energy. I would have thought that seeing the group in the distance would energize me, but it seemed to have the opposite effect. It was almost as if my body said, 'This is close enough. You can rest now.'

Marshall noticed my fatigue, and politely slowed his pace. "You're so close now, Marlee. Just another minute or two, and you can sit then. You made it this far. Keep going." His coaching kept up until we finally reached talking-distance with Sawyer, Ellie and Lydie.

When he saw us, Sawyer jumped up, still favoring his right leg, and awkwardly jogged over to us with a look of confusion and concern. "Did you make it to the ranger station?"

I could not bring myself to look at anyone's face. It was my fault that we did not make it.

Marshall pulled his brother off to the side as Ellie rushed to me, led me to a comfortable looking pile of snow, and sat me down next to Lydie, who was perched on a snow boulder. With a little imagination it could almost be like a beach chair. Okay, with a lot of imagination. Her left leg was braced from the knee to the ankle with two sticks and athletic tape, wrapped around her pant leg. Ellie explained to me that Sawyer told her that with a broken limb, it is imperative to stabilize the bones so that the broken edges do not rub against each other. Apparently that could lead to a medical emergency. With the stabilizing brace, Ellie explained, Lydie should be safe until we found professional help. I nodded, impressed with the medical lesson, and glad that Sawyer seemed to know at least a little bit about wilderness evacuation.

"Today Sawyer hiked to the ridge to check for cell service, but surprise, there isn't any," Ellie said as she stirred food cooking on the backpacking stove that amazingly survived the avalanche. "We haven't really talked yet about what we should do next."

"You look pooped!" Lydie announced.

I met her eyes and began to cry. "Lydie," I sniffed, "I'm so sorry. I just couldn't go any faster and we could see that we weren't going to make it before the sun set. I'm so sorry we didn't find help." I buried my face in my hands and cried. Now how would we find help? Because of me, an entire day was wasted, and the very food that Ellie was preparing now was our only meal. Our supply of gorp was dwindling. At least we had no shortage of water. We could boil snow as long as our fuel for the camp stove lasted, which should be enough for several days. And I figured Sawyer probably had a water filter along too, for pumping water out of streams.

"Marlee, it's okay," Lydie chimed in a cute, sing-songy voice. I smiled then, and Ellie put an arm around my shoulders.

"Actually, Marlee," Ellie stated, "Sawyer and I think

Lydie's leg is not as bad as we thought at first." Lydie proudly nodded her head, making me smile again. "Once we moved her out of the snow, she was able to move it just enough to give us hope that the fracture is not as severe as it looked when we first saw her." Relieved at the news, I took a close look at her leg, and sure enough, she had a tiny bit of mobility, though it hurt her to move it. "We've been keeping her on an anti-inflammatory," Ellie assured me.

Even though Ellie gave a confident impression, I had a hunch that she was far more scared than she was letting show in her face, and I was afraid of what Sawyer would say about our plan now. Thinking of Sawyer reminded me of Marshall's and my conversation on the hike, and now that I was sitting, I felt strong enough to talk.

"So girls," I hushed and leaned toward them, sneaking a look behind me. The boys were still talking about ten feet away. "On our hike, Marshall really opened up and said something that I *have* to share with you." Ellie's and Lydie's eyes widened as if they thought I was going to tell them where buried treasures lie. They were intent on what I was about to share. "I learned that guys are super–"

"Alright girls, time for a conference," Sawyer interrupted. *Not now,* I thought, *this is important.* Not that our plan was not important, but like Marshall confided in me, I needed to warn Ellie to be kind with her words before she said something mean to Sawyer. Based on how peaceful the atmosphere was, I doubted she had lost her temper today. But that was before she knew we were likely not going to be rescued today.

"Later," I quickly whispered and Ellie and Lydie discreetly nodded.

"We have some options to discuss with you," Sawyer announced as he sat at the foot of Lydie's snow boulder. Ellie looked up while still stirring supper and Marshall plopped down next to me, obviously glad to give his feet a break. I smiled and scooted closer to Lydie so we could all talk easier.

"We could attempt to go back to our camp," Marshall said. Sawyer nodded, and Marshall continued, "We are actually closer to where we left our parents than to the ranger station."

That plan sounded good to me! Then Sawyer added, "The only possible problem with that is if our parents left the camp, either in search of us or the ranger station."

We girls silently considered what the boys said. The hike from our parents to here had been fairly strenuous. What if we used all our energy to return to them, only to have them well down the trail in a different direction?

"Another option," Sawyer continued, "would be for me and someone," his eyes scanned between Marshall, Ellie and me, "to again attempt to make it to the ranger station. Tomorrow of course."

We let that option sink in. Yikes. A night in the cold. Another day on the mountain with a small amount of supplies that dwindled every hour. Another day away from medical help for Lydie. That reminded me of Sawyer's leg, and I wondered if he really felt up to hiking.

"And another option," Sawyer stated, "would be to wait here until help comes. Assuming anyone has looked up our location on the satellite messenger, rescuers should have no problem seeing five kids in the area of the buried communicator.

Glancing at each person's face, I suddenly felt Marshall jabbing me in the side. I looked at him, annoyed, but couldn't ignore his urgency. He was watching Ellie with a look of alarm in his eyes. I snuck a peek and saw the reason for his panic. Ellie's face was red and her eyes looked angry. At Sawyer. *Oh, no, I thought, it's just like Marshall said. Once Ellie settled on the thought that we were in this position because of Sawyer's idea, she might launch into him and beat him up, verbally anyway.* I had about one second to stop the inevitable verbal attack.

I jumped up, stood between Ellie and Sawyer, leaned up to Ellie's ear, and whispered assertively, "Girls' conference, now."

I shot a pleading look at Marshall and tilted my head, hoping he would understand. I cleared my throat, "The girls would like to have a short conference now."

Marshall did not look at ease. Had I not just saved the day? Why was he still looking so panicked?

"I don't think there's anything that we girls have to discuss that the boys should not hear," Ellie said in a disgusted tone. I froze. I had to stop her. She marched past me and up to Sawyer, reminding me of the night – just last night, although it seemed so long ago – she listed off all the reasons we should not go along with the midnight hike.

Marshall now jumped to his feet and tried to change the subject by saying, "Now, of course, we should consider weather–" but Ellie ignored him and continued to glare at Sawyer.

Lydie pretended to cough, and then sneeze, and I appreciated her effort to draw Ellie's attention away from Sawyer.

I pulled Ellie's arm and said in a serious tone, "Ellie, I *have* to tell you something." She at least looked at me. "In private," I stated firmly.

Ellie looked perturbed but, to Marshall's and my relief, she shrugged. But before fully turning her attention to me, she frowned again at Sawyer and said in an angry voice, "To be continued."

As I managed to pull her away, my heart raced. *Phew, that was close.* Marshall caught my eye long enough for him to mouth 'Thank you!' at me. I discreetly nodded. Marshall and Sawyer walked about a hundred feet away, and I was thankful for the space, just in case Ellie erupted.

"So," I turned to face Ellie and Lydie, "remember what I started to say, about how Marshall let me in on a very important–"

"Marlee," Ellie interrupted, "I think that whatever middle-school gossip you and Marshall talked about can wait. Right now, we need to figure out what we're going to do, and let's face the fact: we would not be here if it wasn't for Sawyer and his horrible idea to take a midnight hike." *Wow, thanks,* I thought sarcastically. *And I'm not in middle school anymore, but whatever.*

At least she said it to Lydie and me. Knowing my sister, I realized that she probably needed to let this anger off of her chest, but why would she not listen to me? I held up my hand, "I just need a minute of your attention."

Ellie did not stop, "Now you're all buddy-buddy with Marshall, which means that you'll agree with whatever fool plan he and Sawyer come up with next! So you and Marshall bonded today? Well good for you, but I want Sawyer to hear it from me that this is his fault – completely his fault!"

Lydie looked worried. I bit my tongue for the moment, and Ellie continued. "Yeah, Sawyer and I worked well together today, but that was when there was hope of finding help before tonight. The thought of spending a night out in the cold with him is making me feel sick. I'm mad enough to hike through the night to make it back to Mom and Dad."

She seemed to run out of steam, so I carefully began, "Well, while it is true that this idea was Sawyer's, we all agreed to join him. And we were having a great adventure." Lydie nodded and Ellie rolled her eyes. "The truth is, we need Sawyer and Marshall. None of us is as good at orienteering and triangulation as they are. We need their physical strength." Ellie muttered under her breath, but I kept going. "And what I learned today, you know the 'middle-school gossip,'" I shot a look at Ellie, "is that if we smack talk the guys, it hurts them. And when people are hurt, they can't do what they were meant to do. I'm glad you said this to Lydie and me, Ellie, because if you care at all about our family friends, you will not say anything mean or blame Sawyer. We need the guys, so we need to build them up. Be encouraging. Or at least be polite."

Lydie's eyes were big as she took in the lesson. Ellie was listening but did not look convinced. "Or at least be polite," I said again for emphasis. "Please, Ellie, between us three, Marshall told me that guys practically live to impress girls, and that what we say can make or break them. Let's choose to be real friends, to treat them as brothers and esteem them, like we treat each other."

Hearing myself tell Ellie to treat guys kindly stunned me into silence, because right then, an image of my former crush Bentley Bowers and Sierra Wainwright holding hands popped into my mind. I felt like I'd been slapped in the face. And I knew then that being kind does not always come easily.

Lydie brought me back to the present and excitedly matched my new eagerness for The Golden Rule and announced, "I'm in, Sister! I like the idea of being nice to everyone, no matter whose fault this may seem to be. Because, really, this is an adventure no matter how we look at it." Lydie's wisdom is far greater than any other eleven-year-old I know. I beamed at her, then hesitantly looked toward Ellie.

She was looking more convinced and responded, "So, I need to not blame Sawyer?"

"Right," I nodded, holding her gaze.

"And," she paused, "take this adventure as an opportunity to treat him like a brother?"

"Yup!" Lydie said.

"So we got along really well today," Ellie whispered, and Lydie grinned mischievously, "and he didn't annoy me like he usually does." I listened respectfully, even though I wanted to say 'I told you so!' and laugh in her face. "I guess maybe he has matured a lot, and," she looked uncomfortable, "girls, promise you won't breathe a word?" Lydie and I consented, and Ellie pointed at me, "especially you, now that you're all chummy with Marshall." I rolled my eyes and nodded.

Ellie continued, "I keep thinking of Sawyer

differently than I used to. I mean, it's weird, it's almost like I can't stop thinking about him. I hope he thinks I'm helpful enough and strong enough and mature enough and beautiful enough." She blushed when she said beautiful, but then continued, "but sometimes he still just drives me crazy, like going and making those packing lists for us – as if we wouldn't know what to pack ourselves! But then after I blew up at him, I felt really bad. I mean, he's just planning ahead and practicing for when he's a professional guide. I shouldn't have assumed that he thought I didn't know what to pack." Ellie shook her head, and Lydie and I exchanged a knowing wink. Ellie went on, "It's just weird, the way that I feel, I mean. For as long as I can remember, Sawyer has annoyed me, but this summer, I see him as so upright and kind and smart."

"Chivalrous," I piped in. Ellie and Lydie looked at me.

"Huh?" asked Lydie.

Ellie smiled and nodded, "Yes! Chivalrous is a great way to describe Sawyer! Like a knight," she explained to Lydie. "Strong, fights for what is right, polite, especially to girls and ladies," she described.

"Oh, I get it!" said Lydie with a grin.

Lydie was still smiling, and I couldn't help but smile at my big sister. I can imagine that admitting her crush was a big step for Ellie. "Oh, wipe those smiles off your faces, girls!" she teasingly reprimanded. We giggled. "Well, you girls might laugh, but I don't want to have a crush. It was easier when I did not like Sawyer one bit. A crush makes our whole friendship complicated."

"Your whole friendship?" I challenged. As if they had ever considered each other friends before. "Just be kind to Sawyer like you are to everyone else, Ellie," I calmly said. "And everything else you said that you hope he thinks about you, you already are." Ellie hugged me, and I said, "He needs us to trust him. No doubt he is blaming himself anyway, so we need to support him." I felt very relieved that our girls' conference was beneficial. I called to the guys, "The testosterone crew is welcome to return!" They started to jog over to us, and that's when I heard our supper boil over.

6

"Oh, no!" Ellie screeched.

Lydie's eyes were wide. My stomach groaned. Marshall's face was red. Sawyer expertly clipped the handle on the backpacking pot and lifted it off the small stove.

Ellie immediately apologized, "I can't believe I let that happen! I am so sorry," she looked near tears.

Sawyer looked in the pot and quietly said, "It's just a thin layer on the bottom that burned."

"I knew we shouldn't have left the girls in charge of supper," Marshall said with a frustrated scowl.

His sharp response surprised me, considering our earlier conversation, but I figured by now we're all "hangry." So hungry we're angry. Being nice while "hangry" is nearly impossible.

Sawyer looked disappointed, as if he had been expecting a feast and now was given scraps. Ellie slipped away from the group with her hands over her face, and Lydie shot a concerned look after her. I quietly walked the forty feet to her and gently put my arm on her shoulders.

"See, Marlee? This is just one reason I don't want to have a stupid crush. Now I'm like all the other girls my age who start chattering about some boy and then go and mess up something like this! We had one meal! And now we have two-thirds of a meal to split between five ravenous people! All because I was talking about Sawyer," she yelled in a hushed voice.

"Maybe the boys can hunt a deer for us," I said halfheartedly. "Ellie, it's not your fault. I should have been watching the food, too."

She looked up and sniffed back a tear. "I don't want to like Sawyer. I wish he could go back to being immature, and then I wouldn't be so self-conscious around him," she admitted.

"Oh, I see," her dilemma was starting to make sense in my mind. While Ellie may like Sawyer, she didn't want to "like" Sawyer. She didn't want to have a crush on anyone. A crush would distract her from her other aspirations. *Maybe that was part of why she had lashed out at Sawyer,* I pondered. If she was rude to him, and he was rude in response, maybe Ellie hoped that the affectionate thoughts toward Sawyer would stop. I finally understood Ellie's actions.

I heard snow softly crunching behind Ellie and me, and I turned to see Sawyer approaching. I gave her back a little rub and then left to head back to Lydie and Marshall. I smiled at Sawyer, whose face looked nervous as he met Ellie. I watched the two from a distance for just a moment. Ellie raised her head and again apologized. Sawyer, much to my surprise, reached out and put a hand on her elbow. I could see him talking to her, and I wondered what he said, but rather than gawking, I returned to the remains of supper.

"Looks like we'll each get about a quarter-cup of rice!" Lydie happily announced. Lydie could always improve an attitude, and I could see in Marshall's smile that he also appreciated her cheerful outlook. At least it didn't make him madder.

While I knew that a positive perspective would do wonders for our group, I also knew that we needed physical nourishment. Lydie's injured body needed extra nutrients to help her stay strong, and the rest of us would soon wither in this environment. Especially if we planned to hike anywhere tomorrow.

"Marshall," I caught his attention and gestured with my head to meet me a ways out of Lydie's earshot. I needed to ask him a question, but I did not want to worry Lydie.

Before we stopped walking, Marshall said, "Thanks

for stopping Ellie from tearing into my brother. Man, I saw her blood boiling, and I thought if she lit into him, the search party would hear us miles away."

I nodded, "It was a team effort, that's for sure. And thanks again for telling me that stuff about guys," I shyly said. I didn't want him to think I was boy-crazy, but I was glad for the pointers on how to treat my brothers-in-Christ. That's how I thought about boys these days. As brothers-in-Christ. Not that I ever was super boy-crazy, like my best friend Braelynn Gunderson, who has been planning her boyfriend since she was six. But I did like Bentley Bowers for a long time. Did! And I thought he liked me, too. I mean, he held my hand a few times and asked me to dance and just when I thought he really liked me a lot, he asked out Sierra Wainwright. And it hurt. A lot. So now I try not to get crushes.

I again felt humiliated and torn down as the Bentley and Sierra drama replayed in my mind. Before I got to the scene where Bentley asked for his sweatshirt back, the one I still had from the chilly night at the bonfire, Marshall's voice brought me back to the present, though it took me a second to remember that we had been talking about the fight that almost broke out between Sawyer and Ellie.

Marshall smiled, "I knew you would take it seriously. Some girls would use that information to tear us down all the more, but I knew you'd be nice." Hmmm,

Marshall was giving me quite an education. All along I thought girls were the vulnerable ones.

"You said the search party would hear us miles away if Ellie blew up," I quickly said, glancing back to make sure Lydie wasn't listening, "do you think we're going to be rescued? Or is it up to us to hike out?" I watched his face closely as I wanted the plain truth, not a buttered-up version.

His eyebrows slightly furrowed and he looked steadily at my eyes as he stated with a shake of his head, "I really don't know. I wish I did, though. If it is up to us, I think that our best action would be for all five of us to hike out together. No splitting up. Today, we did the right thing to have two stronger hikers look for help, but now we're a whole day later, and we need to get Lydie to a doctor. She still has her perky attitude, but when adrenaline slows and pain sets in, she's going to need help fast." I listened carefully, considering what he was saying. As if he read my mind, he continued, "But, if help is on its way, we need to stay here and conserve our energy and not have umpteen trails leading away from where we are stationed now. Evacuating Lydie won't be easy since we're all so tired and hungry. I'm curious to see what Sawyer has to say."

I nodded grimly, and we simultaneously looked toward Sawyer and Ellie. Ellie laughed and smiled at Sawyer. Marshall smiled and asked me if I had any guesses as to what they were laughing about. "Wow, are those happy people the Ellie and Sawyer we know?" I asked in disbelief.

Marshall laughed and agreed that the change was significant. "They didn't torment each other today," he said optimistically. "Can't help but wonder–" he stopped.

"What?" I asked, knowing full well what he was wondering.

He tilted his head at me, showing that he knew that we shared the thought about Sawyer and Ellie. "Come on, Marlee, I know you've noticed the way they are around each other this trip."

I smiled, "I think it's kind of cute."

"Cute? You girls," he teasingly shook his head. "Cute is a duckling – fuzzy baby animals. Sawyer and Ellie acting all googly-eyed is," he stopped, searching for words.

"Cute?" I suggested with a grin.

Marshall chuckled and gently elbowed me, "We'd better get back to Lydie." I laughed, and we began walking.

"Marshall?" Lydie asked sweetly. I was afraid she was going to ask the same question as me, about whether we were going to be rescued. Marshall nodded at her, indicating to her to continue.

"Tell me the truth, are we–" she was cut off by Sawyer's voice as he and Ellie strolled our way.

"Group conference time!" he announced.

"My question will probably be answered in the conference," Lydie waved her hand at Marshall and me, dismissing her question.

Sawyer and Ellie were walking closely enough to, I couldn't believe I was thinking this, hold hands. *What a crazy thought. Normally the only time they would be that close would be if they were racing.* At least once each summer they did race, and it was usually neck-and-neck. But there was no ruthless competition as they strode toward us. I forced myself to look away and tried to focus on the emergency situation.

But Marshall had noticed, too, and gave me a wink. I stifled a smile, and we turned our attention to Sawyer. Ellie sat down by Lydie on her snow boulder beach chair.

"Does anybody have an exceptionally strong hunch about what we should do, regarding our situation?" Sawyer queried.

Sawyer studied each of our faces, but nobody said a word.

He nodded, and after another moment of silence, said, "There probably is a search for us right now." All of us were visibly encouraged by that statement, and Sawyer continued, "And that almost-certain fact gives me hope that we will be found if we stay right where we are, all of us together." Our response was a collective, affirmative nod.

"Then again," he said in a lower tone, "Lydie needs medical care. And we are almost out of food. This doesn't mean we're going to die, especially since we have drinking water, but we need to plan accordingly." Another collective nod, this one a bit disheartened.

"Assuming a search party is on its way," Marshall asked, "when would you expect them to arrive?"

Sawyer thought for a moment and then began, "Well, let's just say that at 6:00 a.m., our parents realized we were gone. I'm sure Dad noticed that his satellite messenger was gone, and they would be able to tell by the other gear that was missing that we didn't plan to be gone for more than a day. Knowing our dads, they probably figured we attempted a moonlit peak, and from where we camped, this would be the logical peak to summit. It's possible that maybe just our dads headed out looking for us, or maybe they headed toward the ranger station to immediately seek help."

The scenario was growing complex, and I was afraid to hear of any more variables.

"Honestly, I'm surprised they're not here." Four pairs of eyes immediately fixed on Sawyer's face.

Sawyer sat down in the snow and calmly explained, "Our parents probably first discovered our absence around six or seven this morning. Our moms probably freaked out while our dads stayed cool and figured what we were up to. They must know we've all heard their moonlit summit story and would want a similar adventure." All heads nodded in agreement. "So, they probably didn't even begin to worry until at least noon.

Knowing our dads, they may have even climbed the peak to see if they could meet us on the trail, or even see us lower on the mountain. If they went to the peak and saw the damage of the avalanche, they maybe tried to call for help with a cell phone from the peak. But," he paused, "since help is not here yet, I am guessing that they took the more common trail than the exposed ridge we hiked, in which case, they would not see the avalanche or us."

What Sawyer said made sense. Our parents would not automatically assume at our absence that we had taken the quick and difficult ascent to the peak, been caught in an avalanche, and slid a third of the way down the mountain. No wonder nobody was here yet. They probably waited until midday to even consider that we needed help.

"Or," Sawyer continued, "if they hiked to the ranger station, let's again deduce that they would have left camp around noon, the search and rescue team would not deploy until tomorrow morning."

"Except that we don't know that," reminded Marshall. Sawyer nodded grimly.

"What should we do?" asked Lydie.

"Even though we're hungry and exhausted," Sawyer answered, "I think we need to try to hike out. We'll eat our supper, line up our packs like a wind block, hang a bear bag, stoke the fire and huddle close for warmth. First thing in the morning, we'll write a message in the snow with arrows pointing in the direction we'll go in case the rescuers come here, and we'll head toward the ranger station." He gave us a moment to let us consider the plan. "Does anyone disagree?" he asked.

Silence.

Ellie was the first to politely speak. "The truth is, we won't be hiking very fast, considering our circumstances, so if rescuers find our camp, it won't take them long to catch up to us."

"Right," Sawyer agreed. "And, in case rescuers are not coming this way, we'll at least be headed toward help. Slowly, but surely."

More silence. Sawyer asked a blessing for our meal, and I noticed that he thanked God for providing even a small portion for each of us. Sawyer's faith struck me as mature. As we swiftly swallowed our warm rice, we livened up a little.

"So," Sawyer said before a long swallow from his water bottle, "maybe Marlee and Ellie should hang our bear bag while the testosterone crew starts building a snow shelter for us to sleep in."

Ellie and I nodded in agreement and, after washing our pot and spoons clean with snow and gathering the remaining gorp and a handful of granola bars, we told Lydie we'd be back soon and headed down the mountain to find an appropriate tree to hang anything with food smells. As long as we hung the bag a few hundred feet from camp, and all of our "smellables" were in there, bears should not bother us while we slept. Even though we only had a small amount of food left, our cooking gear, chap sticks, and sunscreens would all smell intriguing to a hungry bear. Usually Dad and Caleb use a small diameter rope with a weighted bag on one end to toss over a tree limb and pull up the bear bag. Since we had not packed the parachute cord or the small, sturdy bear bag, we were using Sawyer's brand new climbing rope and Lydie's pack.

Tossing the climbing rope over a tree limb proved to be no easy challenge. We found a rock to tie to the end, which helped the accuracy of our tosses, and eventually would help the rope slip back down to us. After about twenty tries from each of us, the rope finally swung around the ideal limb, about twelve feet up, and five feet from the trunk of the tree. That height and distance from the trunk would make it difficult for a bear to gain access to our bag. When we heaved Lydie's pack containing our smellables up, we made sure to leave it hang about a foot below the branch so small animals, like squirrels, would have a hard time getting in. Ellie tied a reliable taut-line hitch to secure the bear bag. With a high-five for our small accomplishment, we headed back toward Lydie and the boys.

About two steps up the mountain, we heard the huff. Ellie extended her arm in front of my path, stopping me in my tracks. Another powerful sounding huff!

7

We slowly turned and saw a large black bear standing on his back legs, his nose pointed high into the air. Ellie and I knew that black bears do not see as well as people, so often a bear stands on his back legs in an attempt to gather scents and determine what is ahead. He stood about fifty feet from our bear bag, putting him probably seventy-five feet from us.

We watched in horror as the bear hit all fours, stamping the ground with his front paws. This action told us that he was planning to charge. We instinctively reacted by waving our arms high above our heads and shouting. Dad taught us this when we were preschoolers, about the same age that most kids are learning their ABCs. I shouted as loud as I could, and my ears instantly began to hurt from Ellie's deafening hollers. We waved our arms in a panic, trying to appear large and threatening to the bear. Our dad had told us that black bears are rarely aggressive toward people, just hungry and curious. Appearing to be scary would almost always send a black bear in the other direction.

It was imperative that we hold our ground. Running would cause the bear to chase instinctively, like a cat playing with a toy on a string. The instant the "prey" moves, the cat will launch after it like a coiled spring let loose. Dad had firmly taught us that we were never to run from a bear, or any animal, for that matter. I had visualized in my mind how I would handle an encounter like this, but oh, it was tempting to try to escape. I forced myself to keep my feet planted and it took every ounce of self-control to continue facing the bear.

We needed to show the bear that we were not an easy snack and that we were intimidating – even though I was 100% intimidated and terrified! Ellie slowly stooped down and picked up a stick. Extending it above her head she continued to shout and wave her arms. I spread my legs out, making a big X with my body, trying to appear much larger than my 5'7" height. Usually I tire of people telling me, "You're tall for your age," but at that moment I wished I was even taller!

With another huff, the bear shook his head, and my stomach felt as if it hit the ground. He was showing all the signs of preparing to attack us. I begged God to change the bear's mind. Ellie and I kept screaming, even though our voices were growing hoarse. Just when I thought he was going to charge, he turned on his haunches and ran away from us. "That's right, Mr. Bear, you leave us alone!" Ellie called after him. We continued to shout for a minute after he was out of sight down the mountain. His black coat disappeared in the trees. Not being able to see him anymore left a somewhat eerie feeling for Ellie and me. I looked in every direction all at once, squinting my eyes to see his dark coat, feeling paranoid that he would reappear.

Ellie began trembling. I had been trembling since the first huff. We leaned against each other as we tried to steady our breathing. My senses were acutely heightened as I listened and looked for any more signs of the bear. "Let's gather sticks for protection and for the fire and get back to the group," Ellie stammered.

We linked our arms and quickly gathered a bundle of branches, and then, frequently looking over our shoulders, we headed back up, out of the trees and toward our group.

As we emerged from the trees, Sawyer dashed to us. "Are you girls okay?" he demanded, fear etched into his face.

Ellie desperately threw her arms around his shoulders and began to cry. Startled, Sawyer was speechless for a moment, then slowly rubbed her back and addressed me. "What happened?" he quietly asked.

"B–" I started, but was so unsettled that I felt weak.

Sawyer's eyes widened and he slightly released Ellie, put an arm on my shoulders, and sat us down, with him in the middle.

I let out a sob. "You could hear us screaming from camp?"

Sawyer nodded. "Lydie was the first to hear. Marshall stayed with her and I sprinted down faster than my legs have ever moved. So, why were you screaming? What's wrong?"

Ellie was still leaning against Sawyer's shoulder and he reassured us with a string of comforting words. I finally spoke,

"A bear was challenging us."

"He charged at you?" Sawyer looked scared.

"Not quite."

"He bluffed?" Sawyer asked, referring to when a bear charges, but turns away shortly before reaching his challenger.

"Thankfully, no, he did not run at us. But he was huffing, stamping, tossing his head, everything leading up to an attack. Just when I thought he was going to plow into us, he turned and ran away. Down the mountain," I spilled the story, evoking another sob. Sawyer held my shaking shoulders.

We sat there, shaken, for several moments before Sawyer urged, "We need to start back before the sun sets." He helped us to our feet and Ellie's eyes darted around as we began walking, each of us carrying some of the sticks. Sawyer looked guarded but calm.

Trying to lighten the mood, he said, "These sticks will feel nice in tonight's fire."

I forced a smile, frightened by the thought of sleeping out tonight.

"Girls," Sawyer began, "you did everything right. Think about it; the bear might have attacked if you had reacted differently. You scared him so much that he ran away from you. He won't be bothering us again. You handled it perfectly," he assured. Sawyer's statement was true, I supposed, and it did help me feel better. It's not as if black bears stalk people, so now that he thought we were scary, he would be sure to stay clear of us. I prayed. Somehow, I wished this upcoming night was already past.

The hike back to camp seemed to take much longer than when Ellie and I had initially walked down to hang the bear bag. At least our bear bag was far from where we would sleep, though. When we came into hearing range of Lydie and Marshall, Marshall called out, "Everyone okay?"

Sawyer nodded, "Now that Ellie and Marlee scared the pants off an inquisitive bear, we should sleep well tonight."

Lydie's eyes grew huge, "You had an encounter? I wish I would have seen it! Tell me all about it!"

Ellie shook her head, "I'm glad you weren't there,

Lyd. This bear was pretty aggressive. It was all Marlee and I could do to convince him to leave us alone. We thought sure he was going to charge," she said shakily.

Marshall's face erupted into a grin, "Well, good work, girls! You did exactly what you were supposed to do."

Ellie and I nodded, still feeling nervous. I knew that Sawyer and Marshall were right that he likely would not bother us anymore, but I was still scared about sleeping without a tent. This was the only scary bear encounter I'd ever had. I've seen probably a dozen bears in the wild, but never before had one challenged me or acted aggressively. True, the expression in the bear's eyes was fear, but he weighed more than double what Ellie and I weigh together, and he was built to catch and eat food. Black bears do not eat tons of meat, except maybe an occasional calf or fawn, and certainly not people. Still though, if he had attacked, we would have been seriously injured.

Reading my thoughts, Sawyer squeezed Ellie's and my shoulders again and whispered, "God has us under the shadow of His wings. The bear left, didn't he?" We nodded. "And a bear has no reason to go above the tree line. Let's stoke this fire and prepare for bedtime."

Sawyer and I began placing sticks strategically onto the fire while Ellie and Marshall continued to build on the windbreak that the boys had started. Lydie chatted happily, as if we were in the best of circumstances. I was glad for her carefree outlook. It was beyond me how she remained so positive when *she* was the injured one. Thinking of injuries reminded me that when Sawyer met us after the bear encounter, I vaguely noticed his limp returning. No doubt he was overexerting and worsening his injury from the avalanche.

"Careful not to stack them too densely," Sawyer reminded me. "Oxygen has to fuel the fire, so if the branches are too tight, the fire will run out."

"Oh, yeah, thanks. Hey," I lowered my voice, "how are you doing? Your leg?"

Sawyer shrugged, then glanced around to make sure he did not have an audience. "It's pretty sore. I took an anti-inflammatory with supper, but it still bothers me."

Yikes. How would we hike tomorrow? I had figured Sawyer would carry Lydie, but if his leg was that sore, what would we do? "Do you have any idea what it is?" I asked. I wondered what the severity of his injury was.

"I'm no medic," Sawyer said, "but I think it might just be deep muscle bruises. When I was bounding to the ridge to miss the avalanche, I fell and smashed my leg against a rock. I am sure nothing is broken, and I don't think any tendons or ligaments are damaged, but the muscles in my thigh and calf are pretty blue."

I nodded and prayed that he was right that the injury was not more severe than bruising. Sure, it would make hiking difficult, but at least it wouldn't be an injury that would require us to carry him, too. And at least it was not an injury that would haunt him throughout life. Dad talks about an old friend of Grandpa's who suffered an injury to his knee that still caused him pain decades later, even with normal everyday activities. It sounded awful.

Sawyer turned his attention to me, "How are you doing from the avalanche? How is your head? Does anything else hurt?"

Once again, I was reminded of my forehead. I had forgotten about it until I had put on my stocking hat about five minutes ago and bumped it then. My fingers gingerly felt around my forehead, and I winced when I touched the laceration. "I guess it hurts when I touch it, but other than feeling an overall soreness, I think I made it through well."

"Good," Sawyer nodded. "Before we forget again, let's clean that right now. Sawyer walked over to Ellie's pack lined up with the others. "Ellie, may I grab the first aid kit from your pack?" *Wow, good manners.* Ellie also noticed and looked appreciative of his consideration to not just dig right into her bag.

"Of course," she smiled. There it was again. Sawyer and Ellie were smiling at each other. I winked at Lydie. Marshall missed it since he was still absorbed with digging a burrow between two hefty-sized snow boulders with Sawyer's ice axe. Digging with the palm-sized adze end, which is usually used for digging steps into a mountainside, was a slow process. Apparently people who plan to spend time in high-risk avalanche areas carry along shovels; we weren't *that* prepared.

"What a relief that you two are cooperating on this trip!" Lydie announced. I nearly burst out laughing at that. Ellie's face immediately turned red and Sawyer instantly refocused on digging for the first aid kit. He looked like he was trying to act cool and collected, but he had begun furiously plowing through Ellie's pack in search of the first aid supplies.

"Watch it, Sawyer!" Ellie growled. "You're going to mess up my bag." She marched over and stepped in his way, forcing him to move. I saw him grimace and favor his lower leg, but Ellie yanked her pack out of his hands and efficiently located the first aid supplies. "You sure made a mess of this in a hurry," she grumbled. I looked at Lydie, who shook her head and rolled her eyes at Ellie. Marshall noticed what was happening and threw up his hands and looked at me as if to say, 'She was being so nice. What happened?'

I guessed that once Ellie realized that the rest of us noticed them smiling at each other, she became highly self-conscious, and acted angrily, even if she did not intend to act mean. But I could see that the damage was done. Sawyer was now about ten feet away, looking confused and maybe even a little sad. I approached Ellie, thinking that since she was holding the first aid kit she would help with my cut. But she chucked the small zippered pouch at Sawyer and sneered, "Better let him take care of it since he's obviously in charge."

Sawyer ducked as the first aid kit sailed above his head. "Ellie," I scolded, feeling shocked and embarrassed.

"Let her," Sawyer stated, standing up and retrieving the first aid kit. "If that's what she thinks, she might as well say it to my face." There was anger in Sawyer's voice. *Yikes.*

At that moment, Ellie seemed to suddenly remember our earlier conversation, the 'middle-school gossip' talk, and her eyes flashed with pain at the realization of what she had said and done. She shook her head, apology in her eyes, and began, "Sawyer, I'm so sorry. I didn't mean that. I can't believe I just threw a first aid kit at you. I could've hurt you. That would be ironic. To hurt you with the very kit that is intended to heal." She was talking fast now, trying frantically to fix her mistake. But it was clear to the rest of us that Sawyer had been hurt emotionally, and Ellie's rambling would not heal the wound.

Ellie kept on jabbering for a moment before she realized that Sawyer was completely ignoring her, and he had walked about thirty feet away. I wondered what I should do. Ellie knew she had messed up, so I didn't see the need to talk to her. If I went after Sawyer, what would I say? I chose to check in with Lydie.

"Are you comfortable, Lydie? Can I do anything for you?"

She looked upset. "I was only kidding about them getting along. I had no idea she would erupt like that."

"It's not your fault, Lydie. We're all hungry and tired and scared, and people act differently when they're in survival mode. Do you need me to carry you over there so you can, you know, pee before bed?"

She nodded. I summoned Marshall to help me carry my sister. Though she was three years younger and considerably smaller, I was tired enough that I knew I needed help carrying her. Marshall and I each wrapped an arm around her low back, and then braced our other arms underneath her thighs. On the count of three we stood up and carefully carried her off to a somewhat private spot behind a few snow boulders, then left her for a moment. She said her leg felt alright, but Marshall said we would be sure to give her another anti-inflammatory before bedtime.

"I am so sorry that happened," I muttered to Marshall while we waited for Lydie to relieve herself.

He shook his head ruefully, "You can't be responsible for your sister. But hey, at least this time she realizes that she was too gruff. That should help considerably in the future."

I nodded. "Lydie feels awful for trying to tease. She had no idea Ellie would blow up. I think Ellie probably got super self-conscious when she realized that we noticed them smiling at each other. Then her embarrassment came across as anger toward Sawyer. Poor guy."

Marshall gave a half-smile, "He's used to it. Used to her, I mean."

I smirked, "Yeah, that's for sure."

We checked on Lydie and carried her back to our makeshift campsite.

"Let's prop up your leg, Lydie. We need to keep it elevated as much as possible," Marshall said as we started building a sort of snow pillow for her leg. Digging in this snow would have been impossible if not for the ice axes and trowel.

I teased Marshall, "You could be a professional snow sculptor after this trip."

He laughed until Sawyer interrupted, "Good one, Marlee." I slowly turned, hearing a sarcastic tone in his voice. He looked mad and he continued, "Yeah, Marshall could be a snow sculptor after this trip I brought you all on. And you can be a personal counselor. And Lydie can wear a cast for six weeks. And Ellie can keep despising me. And I can forget my plan to earn my mountaineering guide certification. This *trip* was such a terrible idea that I regret ever suggesting it. Can you imagine how disappointed Dad will be when he sees what I did to us? I wish I'd never even dreamt up this *trip*." With that he marched over to the beach chair and hung his head in his hands.

Marshall shrugged as if to tell me that nothing we could say right now would help, so he and I awkwardly worked to situate Lydie for the night. By now the sun had dropped behind the ridge, so daylight was waning quickly. I pulled my stocking hat lower onto my head, flinching when I again bumped the cut. Marshall noticed, but for now we kept trying to help Lydie feel comfortable. By now we had a nice ledge for her leg and we cautiously lifted her lower leg onto the elevated ledge. Lydie held her breath when we moved her leg and it was clear that she was in pain. I again wondered how severe her injury was. Mom and Dad would be sick if they had any idea that their 'littlest lady,' as they called her, was hurt.

Suddenly I heard Sawyer let out a sigh, and I saw him quickly wipe his eyes before turning to me with the first aid kit. "Alright, kiddo, mind if I help you with your forehead?" He seemed almost normal, but I knew he was swallowing many emotions to act so composed.

I nodded and scooted up my hat. He reached up with a pad full of hydrogen peroxide and gently dabbed. I blinked, trying to not appear in as much pain as I felt. Sawyer noticed and asked if I was all right. I shrugged, "I don't know why it has hurt so much the last couple hours."

Suddenly he stopped dabbing and leaned in for a closer look. "Marshall, come here. Bring your headlamp." It was still light enough to see objects easily, but details were dim in the growing darkness. I started to feel nervous when Marshall and Sawyer stared at me with wide eyes, and then Ellie appeared, looking between their heads at mine.

Ellie squinted, and after a moment Sawyer said, "Marlee, it appears that there is a small stick in your cut."

"There's a stick in my head?" I shrieked.

"Well, not a stick. A miniature twig. Only has the diameter of a few pine needles. And maybe two inches long."

"What should we do?" Ellie inquired.

Sawyer thought.

"Let me see!" Lydie said.

Marshall said, "Well it could cause an infection. And tenderness is a symptom of infections, so–"

"But," Sawyer cut in, "if we remove it, it could cause heavy bleeding."

Infection? Heavy bleeding? I vote 'no, thank you, to both.'

Ellie piped up, "Won't cleaning it with peroxide reduce the risk of infection? And by the time an infection would set in, hopefully we'll be back with our parents and would have the means to properly fight the infection."

"So at this point," Sawyer nodded, "blood loss is a greater risk. We have no way to give you stitches, so we need to leave it."

Stitches?! What a relief that they weren't going to give me stitches! I certainly didn't want Sawyer and Ellie and Marshall learning to give stitches, with me as their patient, in the middle of the wilderness.

Sawyer had me take an anti-inflammatory, and noted that our supply in the first aid kit was dwindling rapidly at that rate. Marshall suggested that we start to prepare to huddle up for the night. Marshall explained that the snow walls would protect us from the chilly wind and the cooler night air of the mountains. We would sleep in the trench between two large snow boulders that had settled about six feet from each other. With a tarp draped across the top a few feet above our bodies, we would hopefully stay warm enough to avoid hypothermia. The small fire about five feet from the shelter would also help us. We were all regretting not bringing a survival blanket along. While the daytime temperature had reached close to 70, we anticipated the night temperature to hover just above freezing. I yearned for my cozy sleeping bag.

We began to slowly line up between the fire and the snow shelter that the boys had constructed. Sawyer mildly criticized that it wasn't textbook-perfect, but that he thought it would keep us warm enough. He explained several other styles of snow shelters, and talked about them like an architect might describe styles of houses. It was like watching those interior design shows where the people are weirdly excited about every detail. I tried to listen and nod with interest, but he lost me after snow saw and something about a T-opening. Since our only digging tools were ice axes and a tiny trowel, our snow shelter looked less like an igloo and more like, um, a last-ditch effort. I mean it looked good enough, for sure. Good enough for survival. Basically our walls were two huge snow boulders. Stretched across the top of the walls was a tarp, which was secured in place by, you guessed it, more snow. One end was the mountainside, and the other end was open to the elements. About five feet from the opening was our small fire. Sawyer had built the fire on top of a few boughs from a spruce tree to keep it from sinking into the snow.

Lydie would be in the middle, with her left leg propped on the snow pillow Marshall and I built. To her right side stood Marshall and then Sawyer. Ellie and I lined up on her left side, Ellie on the outside. That way, our two biggest members were on the outsides, in an attempt to maintain warmth.

The five of us exchanged somewhat awkward glances. In any other circumstance, we would make sure the guys and girls had separate sleeping areas. Very separate. Far enough to not smell each other. However, in this situation, huddling together was for survival. We needed each other's body heat if we were going to have any chance.

Miraculously, Sawyer had packed along a second tarp.

For an emergency, he had explained. This constituted an emergency, and the tarp would be a perfect barrier between our bodies and the snow. While the snow would serve as an insulator, our body heat would cause some melting. The slow melt of the snow against our bodies would form ice, which would not insulate us. Thankfully, the tarp would be enough of a barrier to allow for the insulating factor of the snow and simultaneously prevent ice formation.

Without a word, we lay down in the shallow burrow, the tarp crinkling underneath us. The backpacks stood by our heads as a windbreak. I lay on my side and draped an arm over Lydie's waist. Ellie wrapped an arm around my shoulders. Sawyer and Marshall were clumped together. So far it was comfortable, but I wondered how long we could hold these positions.

Lydie announced that it was time for bedtime prayers, and even though it was a little awkward, we each took a turn. I thought it was pretty cool how each of us thanked God for His continued help. We prayed for our parents' peace of mind, for strength to find help tomorrow, and for restful sleep. While we were shy at first, the group-style prayer seemed to re-bond us by the end.

Just as everyone's eyes were drooping, we saw a meteor shoot across the sky above the trees below us. "Awesome!" Ellie whispered. This was only my second shooting star. My first had been with Dad while we were driving one night a few years ago. Awesome was a mild description for what we just saw. A night sky in the unpopulated mountains is very dark, so stars shine like beacons. With the still nearly full moon lighting up the summit and the meteor, I felt like we had just seen the most beautiful sight ever.

I spoke up, "Even though I'm worried about our parents, I'm really glad to be with all of you." I saw Sawyer smile, and the others nodded and added their affirmations. Then I sighed, feeling exhaustion overwhelm me as I let my body settle into the crinkly tarp on the thick snow.

8

___

When I woke up, I mistakenly thought that I had actually slept all night. I felt stiff, as if I had been in the same position for weeks. My head hurt, and I was chilled to the bone. Hoping it was morning, I peeked over Lydie's shoulder and looked for the moon. It was still in the east. I sighed, realizing that I had probably only slept a few hours, meaning that dawn was still hours ahead. Which meant that the temperature would continue to drop for hours before we felt the warmth of the sun again.

Remembering the fire, I saw that it was a small flicker now. I squinted to see if we had any spare firewood. My halfway sitting up caused Ellie to shift. "Shh," I whispered, "just going to check the fire."

She nodded in her sleep, and I slowly crept off the

tarp and tiptoed to the fire. Placing a few more tree branches on it, making sure to leave space between the sticks, I realized that even though I was chilly, my fingers and toes were not numb. In fact, they felt relatively comfortable. I was surprised at how well the snow shelter was working. At first I thought it sounded ironic to try to keep warm with snow, but it did seem to be serving as surprisingly decent insulation.

I heard Ellie whisper, "What time is it?"

Before I could answer, Sawyer quietly called, "About midnight." Startled, I froze in place. I hadn't meant to wake anyone else.

In a moment, Sawyer and Ellie were at my side. "Thanks for tending our furnace," Sawyer graciously said. I smiled and yawned.

Ellie took a step toward Sawyer, and I saw his jaw tighten. Ellie noticed too, and her face showed remorse for her earlier blow up at Sawyer. Unexpectedly, Ellie took hold of his wrist and tentatively asked, "Sawyer, I need to talk to you. Is now a good time?"

I ducked my head and backed toward the shelter. Neither Sawyer nor Ellie acknowledged my departure, but I did hear Sawyer catch his breath when Ellie grabbed his wrist. I was curious to know what she would say, so I hoped they didn't walk out of earshot.

I slipped onto the tarp and wiggled in as close to Lydie as I could.

"I'm sorry," I heard Ellie humbly say. She sounded

sincere, and I decided that she was beginning to understand Marshall's lesson. I just hoped she wasn't learning it too late. "I shouldn't have snapped at you, and I feel horrible that I threw the first aid kit at your head."

I discreetly watched the scene. Sawyer shook his arm free from Ellie's clutch, shook his head and said, "I'm used to it Ellie. Let's just get through this trip together and then I'll stay out of your way."

Yikes. That had to hurt. My heart ached for Ellie, although I couldn't blame Sawyer for his cold reply. I expected Ellie to run off crying or to shove him and give him an earful, but she stayed right where she was. After an icy moment, Sawyer curtly tipped his head at her and began to walk back to our shelter. I hunkered down and closed my eyes, hoping they wouldn't notice my staring.

Suddenly Ellie called out, "Captain," and I heard Sawyer stop walking, but I didn't dare to peek until I heard his boots crunch on the snow as he turned to face her again. When I tentatively opened my eyes a crack, I saw him looking at Ellie, and she took a cautious step toward Sawyer. "Captain," she again said in a hushed voice, and this time he walked to her. My head was spinning wondering what would transpire next.

"I am truly sorry for the mean words I've said to you. I am ashamed that I've thrown a first aid kit and bandana at you. I wish I could take back the mean things I've done to you, Sawyer." When they were standing this close, I could see that Sawyer was about four inches taller. Ellie's pretty brown eyes looked up at him as she spoke. "Sawyer, I would understand if you can't like me after the way I've treated you. But I am going to treat you respectfully from now on. You've been so great on this trip. You're like our backbone, Sawyer. And you've just," she struggled for words, "grown up so much, and I forget you're more of a man and less of a twerp," she said with a playful smile. "I don't want to hurt anyone, Sawyer. I don't want to hurt you." At the close of her last statement, she looked down, as if embarrassed. "I'm sincerely sorry, and I promise to treat you respectfully."

Sawyer, who had been warming his hands in his coat pockets, gently reached for Ellie's hand. My heart jumped to my throat. I heard Sawyer whisper, "I forgive you, Ellie." With that, Ellie looked up at him and grinned. Suddenly, Sawyer stepped toward Ellie and embraced her in a warm hug. I saw him whisper in her ear, and she giggled. When they finally backed out of their hug, Sawyer's hands still on my sister's shoulders, Ellie smiled and said, "Sawyer, I am glad that I agreed to come on this hike with you. Even though the avalanche threw a wrench in the plan, this is quite the adventure, and I'm glad we are in it together."

Sawyer pulled her into another hug and happily said, "Thank you, Ellie. I'm glad you're here, too. And," he added with a grin, "I really like it when we get along with each other."

Ellie beamed and contentedly nodded her head into his shoulder. Wow, was a marriage proposal next? "Thank you for giving me yet another chance, Captain," Ellie said.

"Thanks for looking my past my 'twerpiness' and giving me another chance," he replied with a teasing tone. Ellie grinned up at him, and after a moment I heard Sawyer whisper, "We should really rest now. But I'm glad we had this talk, Ellie."

Ellie smiled again and thanked him for being willing to listen to her apology. Sawyer unwrapped Ellie from his arms, and they walked back to the rest of us. I quickly closed my eyes, but my head was still wide awake wondering about what I had just seen. *What if Sawyer and Ellie get married?* I wondered. In just a few months they would both be eighteen, and it hit me then how close to adulthood we all were – especially Sawyer and Ellie. Marshall and I only had two years left of high school, and Lydie was just three and a half years behind me.

Thinking about the future always feels so uncertain. Some people are so sure of the direction they want to go, yet I have so many interests that I have a hard time narrowing down which path to choose. For now I usually just pray that God will give me clear indicators as to what I should do in the future. The future would come, but as Ellie lay down next to me and snuggled in, I was reminded that at that moment I needed to sleep. I tried to pray, but exhaustion was taking over again.

It didn't take long to slip into a hard, deep sleep. We were all exhausted, physically and mentally, and I was glad that despite the cold and hunger I was able to return to rest. When I awoke again, I heard Marshall and Lydie talking, and I became aware of the sun warming my face. I rolled over, still feeling half asleep. Ellie was still squeezed up against me, though her eyes were open. "Morning, Sister," she said with a smile. I returned her smile, and then yawned and rubbed my eyes. I felt surprisingly refreshed, as if I had just woken from a week-long sleep. I stretched my arms over head and enjoyed the crisp mountain air. Our jackets and hats and packs were all covered in a sparkly coat of frost, but we had survived the night. I knew that the snow blanket and wind break had worked. Even though I felt chilled, I knew that my body temperature was still plenty safe. Without our makeshift shelter and huddle through the night, hypothermia would surely have set in.

Suddenly I heard a symphony of growling stomachs, and as sisters we sat up and looked at the boys. Sawyer was still asleep, but Marshall teasingly said, "The sooner we start hiking, the sooner we eat. I could go for a taco."

I laughed out loud, and I exchanged a smile with

Marshall, who playfully winked. Lydie looked at me inquiringly. I imitated Marshall the best I could by using exaggerated hand gestures and lowering my voice. "I love Mexican food. Any day. Any time. I'm always in the mood for a plateful of enchiladas or burritos." The girls laughed and Marshall grinned.

"Aww, come on, just admit it. At 6 a.m. on an empty stomach, you'd eat a taco right now," Marshall teased.

I nodded, "I would eat a taco right now."

"*A* taco?" he countered. "I would eat seven or eight tacos!"

Our laughing woke up Sawyer, whose eyes instantly looked at Ellie. The two smiled, and I thought that Ellie looked more beautiful than ever before. Somehow even her unwashed, tangled chestnut hair was pretty. Her hair always looks good. On trail, my hair looks unkempt. But not Ellie's. Her face was radiant and her eyes bright. We all needed showers, but her inner beauty shone like the sun. I wondered if Sawyer also saw her as striking. One glance at his face answered my question. He was gazing at her and his cheeks were red, although I wasn't sure if the redness in his face was due to blushing or the cool temperature.

Marshall stretched his arms, cracked his knuckles (which made Lydie cringe), and then announced, "In all seriousness, we probably should break camp and hit the trail. "Girls, you want to retrieve the bear bag?" he teased. Before the scary memory could replay in Ellie's and my minds, he added, "No, no, we'll stick together. Lydie, how are you feeling?"

"Okay," Lydie quietly said which made us all turn and look with concern. "My left leg is just so stiff and sore." She bit back a tear. Ellie hugged her, and confidently said, "We'll do our best to find help as soon as possible."

"We're going to make a stretcher for you, Lydie. You can rest while we find help," Sawyer positively explained.

Lydie's eyes were dull, and I was startled to see her so downcast. Her countenance reminded me that she was in fact injured. When she had remained so upbeat, I entertained the thought that maybe her injury was not severe. Seeing her this morning though, I could tell that she definitely needed medical help. ASAP.

Sawyer's stomach growled, and he rubbed it sheepishly. "Once we retrieve our bear bag, I think we had better eat our gorp to give us some energy for the hike ahead of us." Nobody argued that.

Ellie spoke up, "Marlee and I will help Lydie relieve herself. While we do that, could someone find some moleskin from the first aid kit?"

"You have a blister?" Marshall asked her.

Ellie nodded glumly. Ellie didn't normally have problems with blisters, but once in a while, even the most conditioned skin can blister. Together, she and I carefully scooped up Lydie and carried her away from the boys. Lydie struggled to balance on her right leg, and Ellie and I exchanged an anxious glance.

When we returned to the boys, Sawyer was sitting on the beach chair with the moleskin in hand. "Go ahead and kick off your boot," Sawyer said.

Ellie blushed, "Marlee can do it. Or I can."

"I don't mind, Ellie. I've seen so many blisters that it might be helpful for me to take a look. Just to see how bad it is, and if I need to drain it or not." I cringed when he mentioned draining the blister. Dad always says that it's best to protect a blister and to not drain it. However, if a blister is bound to break open, it's better to drain it than to let it break. Draining a blister, done by carefully poking a sterile needle into the skin along the perimeter of the blister, does not come without pain though. I hoped for Ellie's sake that her blister would be protected by the moleskin, a tough layer of cotton that surrounds the blister, kind of like a tiny inner tube.

"Sawyer," Ellie fidgeted uncomfortably, "umm, my feet, uh, don't smell the best right now."

Sawyer's eyes lit as he suddenly understood why she didn't want his help. "Well," he kindly said, "I doubt your feet smell bad as Marshall's. But if it would make you feel better, I can take off my hiking boots, which would cause you to pass out from their terrible odor, and then you wouldn't even be aware that I was anywhere by your feet. Your non-smelly feet," he added with a smile. I was certain that he was remembering the "Smelly" incident when he said that.

Ellie giggled when he claimed that his feet smelled so bad that it would make her lose consciousness. We all laughed, actually, even Lydie a little bit. Ellie reluctantly untied her boot, and carefully removed her wool sock, then her nylon sock liner. Sock liners move with a hiker's foot, while the sock moves with the boot. The idea is that any friction from hiking will be absorbed between the sock liner and the sock, thereby reducing blisters. Once in a while though, blisters can happen regardless of precautions.

"Pretty good sized, Ellie," Sawyer commented as he held the backside of her heel, looking over her whole foot. Sure enough, on the outside of her right foot toward her heel was a white bubble of skin, about the size of a quarter. She nodded in agreement. Marshall whistled and jokingly asked her if she had gone hiking lately. Lydie grimaced, but I tried to maintain a neutral expression.

Sawyer observed her entire foot carefully for a moment and then asked how her other foot was doing.

"That foot feels fine," she stated, "It's just this that is out of control."

Sawyer nodded, gently pressing on her blister. "Well, as you know, we don't want to drain this unless we think it's going to burst on its own," Ellie nodded as he continued to observe her foot. "I think this one will be okay if you give me a few minutes with the moleskin. We'll try to protect it." Sawyer went to work with the first aid scissors and began to cut a square of moleskin larger than her blister. He then cut out the center of the moleskin, matching the size of the damaged skin, so that the moleskin looked like a tiny inner tube, except with square corners. He carefully positioned it on her foot with the sore skin sticking through the cut-out center of the moleskin. Next he used plenty of athletic tape to help the moleskin stay in place. Wrapping a couple pieces of tape over the edge of the moleskin and then around her ankle and heel, he asked, "Now how does this feel? Supportive without constricting movement?"

Ellie moved her foot around, trying out her range of motion. Nodding with an appreciative smile, she said, "This feels better. Thank you." Sawyer smiled and she replaced her sock liner, sock, and boot.

"It's always better to take care of a blister before it breaks. I'm glad you asked for help," Sawyer affirmed. Marshall noticed their smiling at each other and gave me an inconspicuous wink. He too was amazed by their mutual cooperation this summer. If only he had seen what I had witnessed last night by the fire!

"Next, Marshall and I will hike to tree line and find two tree branches that will serve as poles for Lydie's stretcher. Ellie, stay with Lydie. Marlee, can you write a large message in the snow? Make big block-style letters saying that we're heading toward the ranger station and need medical help."

We all nodded and set about our duties. I had heard Dad talk about fashioning a makeshift stretcher to evacuate a hiker, but I was interested to see how we would actually achieve it with sticks and a tarp. As I began to drag my fist through the top layer of snow, my forehead began to ache with pressure again. I squeezed my eyes shut, realizing that my sudden focus on the reflective snow in the morning light could have triggered a headache. After a moment, I slowly opened them, feeling sluggish. I had a feeling that the day ahead was going to be long and difficult.

9

_____

"HEADING TOWARD RANGER STATION. LEFT AT 0700, TUES. NEED MEDICAL HELP."

I stepped back, admiring my note. The letters weren't all the same size, and in some places they ran together, but overall it was noticeable enough to grab someone's attention and clear enough to convey the most important information.

I was estimating on the time. I had drawn the letters about two feet tall, so that way if a helicopter was on our search, the message should catch someone's eye. Sawyer had instructed me to use block letters, and I think the reason is because straight lines, or geometric shapes, stand out among nature, whose shapes tend to be curvy. I squeezed my eyes closed again. The sun shining off the snow was giving me a headache, even with my sunglasses. Or was it the stick in my forehead? Maybe someday I would laugh about having a stick in my head, but not until the pain stopped. It was causing so much pressure that I desperately wanted it removed. I decided to ask if the group would take it out for me.

Meanwhile, Sawyer, Marshall and Ellie were fabricating Lydie's stretcher. The tarp that Sawyer had in his pack, which served us last night to help keep us from becoming hypothermic, would now serve as an integral part of Lydie's stretcher. Sawyer and Marshall were looking for two long, sturdy tree branches. The plan was to place the sticks parallel to each other on the tarp, slightly wider than Lydie's body. Then we would fold the overhanging sides of the tarp to the center. Lydie's bodyweight, once we positioned her between the sticks, would keep the tarp in place. The four of us would each carry an end of a stick and, God willing, evacuate her to help. Unless help found us first. Between Sawyer's bruised leg and my head, I was feeling extra dependent on God.

"Nice penmanship, Marlee," Lydie teased. I weakly smiled in return. "Are you okay?" Lydie asked.

I squatted, and then sank to my knees, "I just have a headache," I murmured.

Ellie rushed to my side. "You've been drinking water; I doubt you're dehydrated. Could it be hunger?" Ellie had a point there. Often, when I am hungry, a headache starts.

"It feels like pressure in my head, where you all decided I have a stick stuck in my forehead," I told her.

Ellie cradled my jawbones in her hands and looked closely at the wound. "The boys are almost back," I heard Lydie say.

"It's pretty red and swollen," Ellie quietly said. "Maybe we do need to remove it now." I nodded, praying that removing it would alleviate the forceful pressure above my right eyebrow. I was feeling weaker by the minute.

A moment later Sawyer and Marshall were at my side with the first aid kit. The guys helped ease me onto the beach chair snow boulder, and I leaned back, wincing as the sun hit my eyes. Ellie shielded my eyes with her hands, and Lydie passed a water bottle to Ellie, who helped me sip.

"Alright, who wants to actually do the removal?" asked Sawyer. No volunteers. He reluctantly nodded, "Okay, then. I guess I'll do it. Marshall, you be ready with plenty of gauze and peroxide. Ellie, stay by her face and make sure she stays calm and holds still. And while you do that, please hold the headlamp so I can easily see what I'm doing, but without shining it in her eyes. Lydie, please pray."

The delegates immediately did as told, beginning with Lydie's heartfelt prayer over this medical procedure and the coming day, and our parents. I loved how Lydie prayed so confidently, with no fear of embarrassment – just her talking to her Heavenly Father. She inspired me. I think the others thought the same.

"Marlee," Sawyer calmly explained, "I'm going to go about this as if I was removing a sliver, because that's basically what we're dealing with. Since it is a large sliver, it will bleed, so that's why Marshall is ready with gauze. Once we get a handful of gorp in your stomach, you can have a mild pain reliever." I nodded, ready for relief. As Sawyer lifted his hands toward my forehead, I held my breath in an attempt to stay absolutely still.

Out of the corner of my eye, I saw Marshall sterilize a small knife with an alcohol pad. I wasn't supposed to see that, though. Since the twig, or sliver, had apparently gouged under the surface of my forehead, using a tweezers probably wouldn't be enough. I focused hard on Ellie's face so that I wouldn't think about how Sawyer was removing the sliver. I felt a sting, followed by more pressure. I took a breath. Ellie's face was serious and steady. I couldn't see Sawyer's face. I felt a tug, Sawyer impatiently sighed, another sting, then another tug. Ellie's face suddenly relaxed and she smiled. The pressure was immediately less, and I knew that Sawyer was tugging the sliver out. Another small sting, and he held out the tweezers for us all to see the two inch long culprit. Sawyer's estimate that its diameter was only that of a few pine needles was correct. It was the skinniest twig I've ever seen, but after this experience, I knew that it doesn't take much to cause plenty of discomfort.

Lydie whooped for joy, and an instant later, I felt warm blood falling down my forehead. Marshall quickly passed the gauze to Sawyer, who swiftly cleaned the wound and applied compression. I sighed, feeling so much better already. I smiled up at Sawyer, who let out a deep breath.

"Your first backcountry surgery was a success!" cheered Lydie. I guess the excitement was perking her up.

Sawyer lowered his eyes and mumbled, "My first and my last."

Lydie and I looked at him questioningly and he said, in a disgusted tone, "Once my admissions counselor at POGS hears about this, I can say goodbye to my future as a pro guide."

"Why?" I didn't follow what he was saying.

"We'll be all over the news. The reckless kids who carelessly hiked at night and barely survived an avalanche. This will ruin my reputation. Nobody will ever hire me as a guide after this, Marlee." Sawyer looked distressed.

"But why not? Natural disasters happen, and you're guiding us to safety."

Sawyer didn't look convinced, but Marshall spoke up, "Marlee, you can see he's upset about hiking us into an avalanche, and Lydie getting hurt. So just shut up with your cheerleading."

Ouch. Okay, then. Point taken.

Sawyer looked at Marshall with wide eyes. Marshall tightened his jaw and looked away. I didn't realize I had been such an annoying cheerleader. Boys. One minute you think you're on good ground; the next you're told to shut up. Weird! Maybe he was just feeling super "hangry." I was embarrassed, but didn't want to drag down the group, (since apparently I'm a cheerleader, of course), so I forced myself to focus on how much better my head felt.

I let my lungs fill with the clean mountain air, happy to relax my statue-still pose now that a knife was nowhere near my face. My headache nearly vanished, and though I was still famished, the weak and dizzy sensations were already feeling better. As Sawyer taped some clean gauze to my forehead, I actually felt able to hike today. I knew we'd still need God, but now at least hiking felt possible.

"You don't look pale anymore, Marlee," Lydie noted.

I nodded. "I feel tons better. Thank you all so much!"

Sawyer smiled, mischief in his eyes. "Well if POGS is out, maybe I can get into medical school. As long as my medical skills are so strong, what do you say we operate on Lydie now?" Ellie, Lydie, and I giggled.

Marshall rolled his eyes and gave his brother a playful, but surprisingly strong shove on the shoulder.

While the shove was meant to be lighthearted, it caused Sawyer, who was resting his sore leg by my feet on the edge of the beach chair snow boulder, to stumble and flip across the snow chair, making his head and shoulders land in the packed snow. Ellie and Marshall rushed to his side. Lydie and I looked at each other with huge eyes.

"Sorry, man, you okay?" Marshall quickly said.

Ellie was at Sawyer's head in a flash. Sawyer pushed up his upper body with his arms. He looked annoyed and humiliated, but otherwise okay. In a disgusted tone, he grunted and relied heavily on his arms to regain a standing position. His limp leg still hung. Ellie brushed snow off Sawyer's shoulders and hat.

"Sawyer, I didn't try to do that. Man, you just tumbled like a wet noodle. Are ya' okay?" Marshall scrambled for words to apologize.

Sawyer gave his brother a glare and loudly whispered, "Seriously, man? In front of the girls? Come on!" Ellie blushed when he mentioned us girls, and I figured he really meant 'in front of Ellie.'

Marshall looked down.

I was concerned about Sawyer's leg. Not wanting to further embarrass him, though, I resisted asking. I walked a few feet away to where the guys had left the sticks that would serve as the poles for the stretcher. Since each of the two branches had a clean cut, I realized that Sawyer must have a handsaw in his pack.

He sure was prepared! What a miracle that he is our guide, I thought, thanking God for his skill and preparation. The sticks were probably six feet long, and maybe three inches in diameter. They were even reasonably straight, as straight as sticks can be.

I looked back to observe Lydie. I sneaked a fast peek at the rest. Marshall had ambled slightly away from the group and was studying Sawyer's map. Marshall was learning about orienteering and triangulation, which means figuring out a location on a map by looking at landmarks, like peaks or rivers, and using a compass. Dad was trying to teach me too, but it was going to take plenty more practice before I'd be able to find my way with a compass, map, mirror, and protractor.

Meanwhile, Ellie and Sawyer were talking, and Sawyer was lifting up his pant leg. A wave of shock flooded Ellie's face as she checked out his lower leg. I guessed the bruising was awfully bad. Ellie gulped, but Sawyer tried to remain casual. I couldn't hear their conversation, but I deduced that he was reassuring her that his leg was not as painful as it looked. Even though a shove literally knocked him to the ground.

Glancing back to Lydie, I thought of the bravery she was exhibiting through this. I hadn't even seen her break down and cry yet. Maybe she was in a sort of emotional shock and once we found help, or help found us, she would be emotional. While I agreed with what Ellie had said last night, that Sawyer was our backbone,

I recognized that Lydie was a well of positive energy for us. She was the one who was most injured, yet she had remained optimistic through our hunger and fatigue. While it was obvious that her energy and strength were waning, she was still chipper. Watching her now, I could see her face looked pale, and her eyes looked duller than before. They still had their happy spark, except with less vigor. I prayed we made it to help very soon.

Suddenly Marshall was at my side. He wore a guilty expression, as if he were ashamed to return to the group. "Hey," I greeted him, remembering the Golden Rule talk with my sisters. And also slightly remembering how I felt when Bentley slung his arm over Sierra's shoulder in the booth in front of me at Here's the Scoop.

"Marlee, how are you such a peacemaker?" I was surprised by his question.

My eyebrows shot up, wrinkling the tape on my forehead and reminding me that I still had a wound. "Uh," I began, and then paused, "I didn't know I was. A minute ago I was an annoying cheerleader. Usually nobody has a chance to talk when Ellie is around, so maybe I'm just used to keeping my thoughts to myself."

Marshall clenched his jaws. That was not the right thing to say. That probably sounded like I meant that Marshall should keep his thoughts to himself and stay quiet, but that was not what I meant. Well, not exactly.

Unless his thoughts are that well-meaning girls should shut up.

"Sorry, Marshall, that totally came out wrong. Let me try again?" He gave a half smile, much to my relief.

"Okay," I started after a moment of silent thinking, "first of all, thank you for saying that I am a peacemaker. I haven't been told that before, so I appreciate your positive observation." Marshall smiled and nodded, so I felt better about proceeding. "To be honest, I think a good share of it is due to being the middle-born child in my family. So that's nothing I've accomplished. Since I've been a younger sister to Ellie and an older sister to Lydie, I have to be the follower and the leader. And, I mean, I love Ellie. She has so many good traits," I took a breath, hoping that what I was about to say wouldn't be gossip, "but sometimes she does react emotionally. I've seen how that can hurt people, like when she chucks objects at Sawyer, and well, I don't want to be like that." I felt my face grow red, and wondered what Ellie would say if she heard that. Feeling the need to further explain, I continued, "But don't think that I'm perfect at keeping my emotions cool, or that I think I'm better than Ellie, or that I don't want to be like her. I do freak out sometimes, and Ellie has so many traits that I would love to have. Does that make sense? Did I at all answer your question?" I was talking fast and my thoughts seemed all jumbled up.

Marshall nodded, "So basically, you follow the good example, use the bad example to help yourself be better, and don't throw stuff at people?"

I smiled. Now that he summarized my monologue, it sounded clearer. "I think so. But I pray every single day to treat people well. It's such an ongoing battle."

Marshall had an incredulous look. "You?" he sounded shocked. "Marlee, you're pretty much my role model for how to treat people. I had no idea that you struggle with keeping your emotions in check!"

I was stunned. *I am a role model?* I mused. *He thinks I treat people well?* I was touched by the compliment, but before arrogant thoughts multiplied, I knew that I had God to thank.

"You know Marshall," I said after a moment, "this is the first summer that I have really gotten to know you."

"Yeah, it's best when I keep quiet," he murmured.

I tilted my head, silently asking him to elaborate on his thought.

"I do such stupid stuff, Marlee. Like dumping my pack. Telling to you shut up. I'm sorry, by the way," he murmured. I nodded and he continued, "Shoving my injured brother in front of the girl he has a major crush on. That's between you and me," he quickly added with wide eyes, as if he had been sworn to secrecy and accidentally spilled the news. I giggled with a nod. He looked frustrated with himself and continued, "I forgot to carry your pack when you had a stick in your head.

And that's just in the last few days. Marlee, compared to Sawyer, I feel like such a mess up. If I could be half as successful as him, I'd be a hundred times better than I am now. I'm just little Marshall who tags along in Sawyer's shadow, but he will always outshine me. Anything I try to do, Sawyer has already done, and done much better than I'll ever do." He shook his head and finished his self-attack.

I sighed, feeling surprised at how hard he was on himself. I was unsure of how to encourage him. Suddenly, a thought popped in my head, and I sure hoped it was from God. "Marshall," I said slowly and he looked at me, "what would you say if I said all that negative stuff about *myself?*"

He shrugged, "Well it wouldn't be true, and I would say that you were being too hard on yourself."

I nodded, "Interesting."

"What?" Marshall prodded.

"Marshall, I think you treat other people well. Most of the time," I added with a half smile. "Give yourself a break. If you hiked all day in my boots, you could find plenty of errors. But you're not attacking me about them. Don't attack yourself either. Lighten up."

He silently considered our conversation as Ellie and Sawyer approached. They were talking happily to each other as they walked toward us. Sawyer's limp was not any worse than before, but it was noticeable. Before anyone could ask how he was doing, he called out, "Let's pack up and head toward the ranger station."

Marshall and I squatted down to carry the sticks to Lydie. She held up the tarp with a faint smile. "This twenty dollar tarp is turning out to be a lifesaver!" We all smiled at her.

"Good thing Marshall insisted that I pack it," Sawyer stated. We girls turned to face Sawyer who was looking at Marshall. Marshall gave a slight smile, but his eyes shone with pride. "That's right," Sawyer continued, "I said we wouldn't need a tarp for this trip, but Marshall insisted. Turns out he was very right. And I'm very glad you insisted, Brother," he said with a nod to Marshall.

Marshall smiled. "Good work, Marsh," I said.

"Yeah, thanks a ton, Marshall," Lydie piped up. "Without your preparation, I wouldn't experience the flying tarp ride."

We laughed again before Sawyer said, "Well, we probably could have figured out a catapult system to launch you to the ranger station. But, after this, I'll always have a tarp along."

I thought that Sawyer's public compliment would surely boost Marshall's spirits. I hoped so anyway. I think it's sad when people are so negative. Certainly self-discipline can be helpful, but not when it is so harsh that it prevents a person from thriving. Anyway, I hoped that Marshall would begin to see himself as capable and worthy of respect.

10

"How does it feel, Lydie?" Ellie asked. Sawyer and Marshall had just set Lydie on the makeshift stretcher, and we were beginning to lift the branches to test it in action.

"So far, so good," Lydie gave a thumbs-up.

"Does it feel like the tarp will stay in place, or is it slipping out from under you? The last thing we want is you falling," Sawyer said as we continued holding her just above the snow.

"It feels pretty secure right now. Believe me, Sawyer, I'll scream if I feel it slipping," Lydie said with a smile.

"Okay, then. Ready, Pals?" Sawyer asked.

"Ready," four voices called back to him.

"Onward," he said, "I think it'll take us awhile to find a pace that works for all of us. For now, we need to communicate. Slower, you two," Sawyer told Marshall and me. Ellie and Sawyer were in the front, on the downhill side. Marshall and I were in back, by Lydie's head, on the uphill side. We decided that having a guy on each end would help Ellie and me, since the guys are stronger. We also thought that since Sawyer and Ellie are the tallest two, they should be on the downhill side. Lydie smiled up at me as Marshall and I slowed our steps.

Sawyer had rigged up a system with his climbing rope in which the rope was tied to Marshall's and my ends of the stretcher poles. We slung the rope over our shoulders and held onto the rope with our hands at waist level. Lydie's head was at about my knee height, mostly level with her feet, which were up by Sawyer's and Ellie's waists. The setup was to help keep Lydie level. Otherwise, at the steep angle of the mountain side, she would be insecure on the stretcher riding at a 45 degree angle. The remaining 160 feet of climbing rope was neatly coiled on her lap.

With the four of us working together, Lydie and the rope were pretty light. However, my clutch on the ropes felt uncomfortable and I was so hungry that my stomach panged. I was glad that Sawyer had given me a pair of leather gloves to wear. I had winter gloves along in my pack, but it would be difficult to grip tightly enough with the bulky thermal gloves. Marshall had graciously offered to carry my pack, which I appreciated. I could hear his stomach growling, though, so I figured by mid-morning I should offer to take a turn. Right now I had Lydie's pack on my back, but it weighed considerably less than mine.

"I'm fine with this pace," Ellie said, "Should we go a bit quicker?"

Sawyer hesitated, "Maybe when we find the trail." Ellie shrugged, glanced at his limp, and continued at the slower pace.

I glanced at Marshall. He seemed to be mostly comfortable. As usual, I figured he'd be stronger physically than me, and this task was proving so. I already felt winded, and the rope pressing on my shoulders hurt. I had replaced my warm jacket with a light sweater before we left. Though the air was still crisp, we would heat up quickly now that we were hiking. And the lower we went on the mountain, the higher the temperature would be. I always thought that seemed backward, since usually heat rises. Dad explained to me that oxygen is less dense at higher elevations, and it is the oxygen that has the ability to hold heat. So, as the oxygen density decreases, so does the temperature.

Right now I wondered if I could adjust the climbing rope to rest on the shoulder straps of Lydie's pack on my back, so the rope wouldn't rub my shoulders. I almost asked the group if we could stop, even though we had just begun, but then I saw Lydie's hopeful and admiring countenance. She was looking at me as if I had just won the Nobel Peace Prize. Her gaze invigorated me, and I made a strong effort to ignore the rope pinching my shoulders.

The only sounds were our breaths and our boots crunching in the snow. And the occasional growling stomach. It was kind of serene in a way. I mean, if I looked past the fact that we were evacuating my sister, and our parents were probably frantic. Suddenly, Lydie spoke up, "I just love you all. Seriously, you're carrying me on a tarp!" she declared with a smile.

We smiled. Ellie and I affirmed that we loved her too, and even Sawyer said, "Aww, you too, kiddo." Marshall just gave an awkward smile.

"Really, thanks for carrying me like this," Lydie stated.

"It's a medical evacuation, actually," Marshall said with a teasing smile. And on we went.

Twenty minutes later, we were still struggling to find a comfortable pace. Ellie visibly restrained herself from going faster, and she made it clear to us that she was frustrated with the slow speed by loudly sighing every few minutes. Sawyer shuffled along steadily, almost dragging his aching right leg. Marshall seemed comfortable enough, and I had discovered that by shifting the rope slightly, it weighed down on my muscle rather than my bone. For now it was working.

"Can you two in the back go any faster?" Ellie asked.

Her voice sounded polite, but given the circumstances, it was rude. I wondered with disgust how she could even consider asking that aloud when it was clear that Sawyer was in considerable pain.

Not wanting to embarrass his brother again by reminding her of Sawyer's leg, Marshall gritted between his teeth, "If we take longer strides, our legs will bump Lydie's head."

Ellie sighed again, "I'm just concerned about getting Lydie to help ASAP. Maybe you could keep your strides the same length, but take more steps?"

That made me mad. Usually Ellie doesn't make me downright angry, but that last comment did. My face heated and I opened my mouth to give her a piece of my mind. I wasn't sure just what would come out of my mouth, but I could not listen to her complain in this situation.

Suddenly, before I vented, in a sweet voice, Lydie said, "Ellie, I feel alright. I am comfortable for now, and I think it's better if you four just keep up this pace. If you push the pace too much on empty stomachs, we'll all need medical help." Leave it to Lydie to settle the disagreement.

Lydie had spoken just in time to prevent me from really causing steam in the group. I silently thanked God for her timely comment. I made a mental note to tell Marshall later that I had nearly had an emotional outburst. It might be encouraging to him to know that it takes endless effort to keep my emotions in check.

I glanced at Marshall and he gave me a look that made me think he could read my mind. Without a word, he tilted his head toward Sawyer, and then shook his head with a frustrated look toward Ellie. He too was angered that Ellie suggested increasing our speed with Sawyer's condition. He did seem to be traveling steadily, though. I figured it was taking substantial mental power to keep himself going.

My thoughts trailed to my mom. If she were here with us, I had no doubt that she would stay calm and keep the rest of us composed, too. It pained me to think of how terrified she must be, wondering about us. While we kids certainly have had an adventure, thinking about Mom made me regret going on this excursion. Last night while lying beneath the glittery stars, I decided I was glad to have agreed to join the others on this hike. But suddenly, the realization that our parents would have been distressed for over 24 hours made me feel sick and ashamed at my decision.

Perhaps the most disquieting thought was that if we had asked permission to go on our trek, our dads probably would have accompanied us rather than not allowing us to go at all. In my mind's eye I could see Dad and Caleb hiking with us now, evacuating Lydie together. Dad would be so gentle with Lydie, and he would clap Sawyer on the back and bump Marshall's shoulder, telling us that we are going to be just fine. He always knows just how to handle Ellie's emotions. He gives her space when she needs space, and he hugs her when he senses that she needs him close. He would give me that smile that reassures me – the same smile he gave me after I fell off a horse at my riding lesson. Dad's smile silently tells me that God is my strength.

I began to tear up thinking about my wonderful parents. Suddenly a tear slipped down my cheek, but because I was holding onto the rope that supported Lydie's stretcher with both hands, I was unable to wipe the tear. As I rubbed my cheek on my shoulder, I noticed Marshall giving me a look of concern. I forced a smile, hoping he wouldn't ask what was wrong – at least not in front of the group.

I mouthed, "I'm okay," to him, and he nodded. He probably figured out that some girls cry pretty easily – especially tired, hungry, lost, and hurt girls. That was fine with me. For now, I'd distract myself with thoughts other than my parents. When I was back in their arms, and we knew Lydie was on the road to recovery, I could let my tears flow. But while enroute to help, I had to be strong. *God, please give me strength.*

That's when I noticed a bird chirping. If we were home in the Midwest, a singing bird wouldn't normally grab my attention. But above tree line? Wait a minute. Looking around me, I became aware of the scattered trees right next to us. And they grew thicker up ahead.

I realized that we were no longer crunching on packed snow. Instead, we were on a dry covering of dirt and pine needles. How had I not noticed our entrance back to tree line? The lack of nourishment was definitely affecting me and affecting all of us. At least we were plenty hydrated. Above tree line, we had boiled many liters of water, enough for each person to have three whole water bottles. It made for lots of weight to carry, but like Dad always reminds us, water is life. Even so, I knew enough that if we didn't take in some nourishment, especially electrolytes, we would all wilt quickly. We'd been weakening for a day already. From here out, we'd get worse much faster.

My thoughts jolted when Sawyer stumbled. One moment we were moving right along, and the next, Sawyer was on his knees and Lydie's foot end of the stretcher was planted on the ground.

"Whoa!" Wind rushed out of Lydie's mouth, surprised as all of us. Thankfully, Ellie reached back and prevented her hurt leg from hitting the ground.

"Sorry," Sawyer murmured as he struggled to stand.

"We should take a break anyway," I offered. Obviously Sawyer needed one. We might as well stop since we already were.

Ellie whipped around, her eyes brimming with tears. I was shocked to see her crying. I expected her to be mad.

"Lydie, are you okay if we set you down?" Marshall asked. Lydie nodded, looking worriedly at Sawyer.

On the count of three, Marshall and I eased her head down. When the rope relaxed on my shoulders, I breathed a huge breath. I suddenly felt weightless – almost how I had felt when Marshall first dug me out of the snow.

I glanced toward Sawyer, but decided to give him a minute with his brother. Ellie had walked off the trail about ten feet and buried her head in her gloved hands.

"Hey, El," I gently said. Without looking up, she held out an arm for me to join her. Resting a hand on her shoulder, I squatted down beside her, my thigh muscles burning. Dad always says hiking downhill is harder than hiking uphill.

Ellie sighed and, as if reading my mind, said, "We need Mom and Dad."

I nodded, tears once again filling my eyes. "Soon," I stated as the tears started to drip onto my face.

Ellie hugged me and, to my surprise, said, "You have been so strong on this adventure. I'm proud of you, Marlee."

I hugged her too and held back a sob. Her praise meant tons to me. Sometimes I feel like Marshall when he said he feels that he'll never be as accomplished as Sawyer. When Ellie called me strong and showed pride in me, I felt rejuvenated – I mean, still hungry and weak, but stronger mentally, at least. And sometimes mental strength is the most crucial part of survival.

I grinned and quietly said, "Let's go check on your–," I caught myself, "Sawyer."

Ellie gave a shy smile and nodded.

"By the way," I added, "Kudos to you too, Ellie. You've been pretty great on the trip."

Walking back to the trail, we saw Lydie sitting up, sipping water from her bottle. Marshall was holding a water bottle for Sawyer as he slowly crunched the very last of our gorp supply. The last precious handful of calories. Maybe we could dig up some roots like the ancient Native Americans. When we approached, Marshall backed up and handed the water bottle to Ellie, intuitively knowing that she would want to take a turn helping Sawyer.

"You mind helping him while I grab some water for myself?" Marshall asked Ellie. She smiled and took the bottle. Squatting down, she looked into Sawyer's face. I held back, unsure what to do. Deciding to observe my sister and Sawyer for a minute before taking a drink myself, I quietly acted casual about five feet away. I think we were all secretly spying on Sawyer and Ellie.

"My leg just stopped," Sawyer quietly said.

Ellie cocked her head, inquiring for more information.

"It feels like pain is radiating every direction from this spot," he pointed to a spot on his mid-shin, "but I've been able to hike through it. But just now, it simply wouldn't go. My mind couldn't make my leg go," he shook his head, sounding scared and disappointed in himself.

Ellie rested a hand on his shoulder, maybe to keep them both calm. I fretfully wondered what was wrong with his leg. What if Sawyer's leg was broken too?

"Let's prop your leg up while we rest here," Ellie diplomatically said as she reached for a couple backpacks. "Lean against this log, and we'll support your leg above your heart." She helped him to the nearby downed log, and I joined her to arrange the packs to make a comfy foot rest for him.

Ellie frowned, "Let's take your boots off, too."

Now it was Sawyer's turn to cock his head in inquiry. Ellie looked serious, so he shrugged and untied the laces, cringing as he pulled the boot off his right foot. Ellie is super interested in human anatomy and physiology, and I know that she reads about health stuff all the time. She wants to work in the medical field, and she even job shadows with our local vet, so even though she is only seventeen, with all the research she has done, I knew she had a reason for asking Sawyer to take off his boot.

"What else have you been doing this summer, Sawyer?" she politely inquired.

Sawyer studied her face and after a moment answered, "Preparing for this trip."

Ellie smiled. "I should've said it this way: what kind

of physical training have you been doing lately? Running? Lifting weights?"

"Uh," he hesitated, as if embarrassed, "I've been running with a weighted pack up and down the bleachers at the football field. And pushups and stuff. I've been trying to climb the ladder on my neighbor's silo with just my arms."

Ellie nodded, obviously impressed. I was pretty much floored. Sawyer had been training much more vigorously than any of us girls had. I mean, we went on walks and slow runs and hiked up and down a large hill with packs. But running up and down bleachers? Pulling his body weight up a sixty-foot ladder with his arms? That was hard core! He must be totally ripped – probably like the cement-pouring construction guys.

"Have you ever had shin splints before?" Ellie asked.

Sawyer shrugged, "Not that I know of, I guess."

"Hmm," started Ellie, "do the muscles in your shins ever hurt?"

Sawyer gave a nod. "Now that you mention it, I guess they had been sore lately. I didn't realize it was a problem though. I just figured it was muscle soreness."

"To my knowledge," Ellie explained, "shin splints basically refers to muscle soreness, but if it goes on too long, you could develop a stress fracture."

Sawyer's eyes widened.

"For now," Ellie calmly said, "I'm going to try to tape

your lower leg. It can support the muscles and help get you to help."

"You're helping," Sawyer nicely said.

"Professional help," Ellie clarified with a nod.

"Why did you want me to take off my boot? Are you gauging my level of stink with some kind of odor-meter?" he suspiciously asked.

Ellie laughed. "Actually, there is a condition called compartment syndrome that can be quite serious, but I don't think you have that. But if you did, any compression on your lower leg or foot could worsen the condition. Again, I don't think you have that." She rattled all this off as easily as if she were explaining how to make a peanut butter sandwich. Wow!

Sawyer's eyes were wide as he gazed at Ellie with a look of awe. I think he was as amazed at Ellie's knowledge as she was at his physical training.

"I need the first aid kit," Ellie suddenly said.

Sawyer and I looked at her. "It's under your foot," she quietly said.

"Oh, yeah," Sawyer quickly said as he moved his leg off the pile of packs. "So, where did you learn all this medical knowledge?"

Ellie shrugged, "Reading, I guess."

Sawyer laughed. "I read too, but my backpacking magazines don't cover all this."

Ellie smiled. "I've also learned tons at the vet clinic."

"Treating me like a dog," Sawyer playfully said and shook his head.

"It's a large animal vet clinic," Ellie corrected.

"Treating me like a sheep," he tried again with the same level of humor in his voice.

"You smell like one!" Marshall called from where he and Lydie waited.

"You hike like one," Ellie kindly offered. All eyes turned to Ellie, and she quickly added, "Those mountain sheep we saw the other day were as spry and sure-footed as any creature I've ever seen."

Sawyer's eyes were fixed on Ellie and his face glowed from her praise. "I'll take that as a compliment." Watching them look at each other reminded me of last night by the fire. They wore the same smiles and the same sincere expressions. Maybe Marshall was right that cute wasn't the best word to describe them. Amazing. Revolutionized. New and improved. Still, definitely cute.

Ellie reached for a roll of pre-wrap and a roll of tape from the first aid kit. While she busied herself with taping up Sawyer's lower leg, I excused myself to check on Lydie. I found her dozing in the warm sunlight, leaning against a tree. Marshall must have helped her move off the stretcher. I glanced around, and when I didn't see Marshall, I figured he had walked off trail to relieve himself. Noticing that the stretcher needed to be re-folded, I began to straighten it, but the sight of Lydie with the sun lighting her face stopped me.

Lydia Joy, I thought. I remembered the day she was born. I recalled Dad picking Ellie and me up from Grandpa and Grandma's to go meet "our baby." The whole drive to the hospital, Dad wouldn't tell us if we had a brother or sister. He never gave us a hint. He was so excited to surprise us that he took a picture of our faces as we walked into Mom's hospital room behind him and took in the pink hat and blanket. We were perfectly elated with a sister. Mom told us her name was Lydia Joy, and, while I don't remember this detail, I enthusiastically introduced my baby sister to the nurse as Lydie. The nickname stuck, and she's been Lydie ever since.

When did she grow up? I pondered as I observed how long her legs suddenly looked. I also noticed a fresh sprinkling of freckles under her eyes. I smiled as I thought of her chipper attitude. For only eleven, Lydie was very wise. For the first time, looking at Lydie, I saw a strong resemblance to our mom. Mom. A pang of longing for my mom hit me, and I caught my breath.

"You okay?" Marshall's voice surprised me.

"Yeah, I was going to tidy up the stretcher," I quickly said. Back to business. I quickly prayed that I would be back with my parents later today. "I could use a hand, though."

Marshall nodded and stooped down to reposition the

sticks. "How is Lydie?" I tentatively asked. "Did she talk at all before she fell asleep?"

Shrugging, he explained, "I think she's in a lot more pain than we're aware of, and her body is just exhausted. It's good she's able to sleep some. I just wish we could get her to a real doctor sooner."

"Do you know how close to the ranger station we are?" I optimistically wondered.

"More like how far from the ranger station we are," Marshall dryly answered.

My eyes shot to his face. We had been hiking for about three hours, I determined from checking the sun's height in the sky. I glanced up to double check. *Yup, it's about 10:30.* And while I had lost track of how long we had been on the trail below tree line, I thought we were already farther than Marshall and I had made it yesterday.

"Marlee, all things considered, we're making decent progress. Keeping in mind that none of us has had a real meal for a day and a half, Sawyer has a bum leg and we're evacuating Lydie, we're doing well. But we still have three miles ahead of us," he explained.

To say I was disappointed at this information is an understatement. Chewing my lip, I forced myself not to cry. *Think of the steady progress. Stay calm. We're doing fine. Dad and Caleb are probably helping the Search and Rescue Team, and Mom and Julia are probably preparing warm food for us.*

"Hey, it's okay, Marlee." I jumped when I realized Marshall had figured out my train of thought.

Meeting his eyes, then glancing again at Lydie, I whispered, "Do you really think so? When do you think we'll be back with our parents? How long until Lydie can get to a clinic?"

"We're in Colorado, Marlee, not Timbuktu! Remember what Sawyer said yesterday. By the time our parents realized we needed help, the Search and Rescue Team probably just took action this morning. Obviously I can't say for certain, but I really think we'll either be found or get ourselves to help by tonight," Marshall encouraged.

"In time for supper?" I hopefully asked.

Marshall playfully bobbed his eyebrows up and down. "Pretty sure our moms planned burritos for tonight's supper."

Laughter erupted out of me. Maybe it was the hunger and fatigue mixed with the stress of the unusual last two days, but regardless, I laughed uncontrollably and had to drop to my knees. *Marshall and his Mexican food!* My stomach muscles started to ache from hysterical laughing. "You–" I tried to say, but was cut off by my own giggle.

Swallowing a couple more giggles, I tried again, "You sure don't want to be late for that meal!"

Marshall was doubled over laughing too, but between fits of laughter, he managed to say, "It's the best food anywhere, especially when your mom dices up jalapenos."

"It is good," I agreed with him, "but I never knew food could be such a motivator!" I took a few breaths as the laughter subsided. "Wow, I'm not sure why that struck me as so hilarious, but it sure was good to laugh!"

Marshall's laughter dwindled into a final chuckle and he nodded his head, "Yeah, laughing is good."

"What's so funny over there?" Sawyer called.

Marshall erupted again, and I supported my tired abdominal muscles with a hand. Hunching over, I socked Marshall's shoulder and then made my way over to Sawyer and Ellie.

"Burrito night," I finally squeaked in explanation. "Marshall is hoping we make it in time for our moms' burritos."

Sawyer threw his head back in laugher, and Ellie shook her head with an amused smile. "Here we are stranded on the side of a mountain with two injured hikers, and your priority is supper?" Ellie teased.

"Food is my motivator. Hey, I'm growing!" Marshall shrugged with a comical glint in his eyes. Changing topic with a tilt of his head, Marshall asked Ellie, "What did you do to Sawyer's leg? It looks like you built him a cast."

Ellie nicely explained that by wrapping his lower leg with tape, she hoped to provide support for his fatiguing muscles. "We don't want the injury to progress, so I hope this works," she added quietly. I could tell from her tone she was worried that Sawyer might soon be in a similar condition to Lydie.

Wanting to lighten the mood, I suggested, "Maybe you could tape Marshall's stomach until we get some supper in him."

"Now you're talking!" Marshall exclaimed. Sawyer and Ellie cracked up and Marshall jokingly reached for the tape.

After another minute, Sawyer pointed to the topographic map draped across his lap. "We camped here," tapping his finger to show us, "and we're here now," he said as he dragged his finger about six inches on the quadrant. "The ranger station is there, and it's 11:05 right now. If we can continue at the pace we had this morning, I think we will arrive about 4:00 this afternoon."

"Do you think we can continue the same pace, Bro? Seriously, is your leg up to it?" Marshall quietly inquired.

"All I can do is pray and keep taking one step at a time," Sawyer squarely said. "But I have to keep going. I will do everything in my power to get you girls back to your parents, and Lydie to the hospital. When this is all over, I'll kick myself for years to come for dragging you into this dangerous scenario. But right now, my focus is getting you to safety. I should never have brought us on this–" he was cut short by Ellie, who gently placed a hand on Sawyer's shoulder.

"Sawyer, we wanted to come. We agreed to join you. Don't beat yourself up over this. I'll even tell your parents that the natural consequences of the avalanche have been a suitable enough discipline and no further reprimands are necessary," Marshall and I laughed at Ellie's determination of how Sawyer should be punished for his idea of our moonlit summit. *Wow. Ellie had her perfect opportunity to chew out Sawyer, but she chose to build him up instead. Good going, Sis!* I thought.

Based on the rapport between Ellie and Sawyer the last two days, I expected him to gaze at her again, but instead he hung his head and was silent.

Deciding I should check on Lydie and give Sawyer some space, I rubbed his shoulder in a sisterly way and said, "Captain, I'm going to check on Lydie. Whenever we need to load up again and go, let me know and I'll wake her."

I wondered what Sawyer was thinking. Did he feel unworthy now to be called Captain? Was he mad at himself? Disappointed in us? I didn't have a clue how to handle his emotions, so as I made my way toward Lydie, I was relieved when Marshall joined me so I could ask him.

"Was that totally the wrong thing to say, Marshall? Did I sound sarcastic? Do you think I made him feel like a failure? I was trying to build him up, but what if I came across as patronizing?" I quickly asked.

Marshall shook his head, "No, Marlee. Actually I came to thank you for handling that perfectly. You knew that he needed space, and you knew that he needed to hear something positive. You said just the right thing, as always."

"Phew, am I glad to hear that. Thanks," I sighed.

About eight feet in front of us, Lydie stirred in her sleep, so we stopped walking and looked at each other. "Marlee," whispered Marshall, "can I tell you something?" I noticed for the first time that Marshall's eyes looked dull, not as much as Lydie's, but concern washed over me.

"Anything," I nodded.

"Please don't worry. But someone needs to know that I'm not doing very well. Remember how you were yesterday? Headache, weak? I feel like I'm beginning to reach that point now," Marshall confided.

As he spoke, his expression reminded me of how I felt yesterday before the stick was removed from my head. "We really should have packed more electrolytes," I muttered in frustration. "Let me ask Ellie if we have any electrolyte solutions in the first aid kit," I rapidly thought.

I figured Marshall would stop me, so when he slouched against a tree near Lydie, I realized how quickly he was deteriorating. It couldn't have been 15 minutes ago we were laughing our heads off about burritos, and now he was weakening faster than a flower wilting in the hot sun.

"Hey, El," I said as I returned to her and Sawyer, who was looking a bit perkier, "I wondered if we have any electrolyte solutions in the first aid kit. I just thought with no food or snacks, we should probably each have some." *I sounded so calm that I surprised myself.* I felt like God had put the words and easy tone in my mouth for me.

Ellie mock-slapped her forehead, "I can't believe I didn't think of that! How stupid! I should have had us all take some first thing this morning!"

Now it was Sawyer's turn to encourage. "You probably did think of it, but decided to wait until the last resort. You're right, Marlee, we should each have electrolytes. I'll test out my taped leg, hope it works better than the action figure from my fifth birthday when his leg had to be taped, and mix each of us a liter." Ellie and I smiled when he mentioned the broken toy, and I watched in awe as he practiced standing on his sore leg and gathered water bottles. He sure was strong, physically and spiritually.

One glance at Ellie told me that she was thinking the same thing. It was exciting to see Sawyer and Ellie working together so well, and even admiring each other! I playfully elbowed her and waggled my eyebrows, which made her blush and fight a smile.

A moment later Sawyer delivered us two bottles with the electrolyte solution mixed into our water. I intended to slowly sip on the mineral-loaded water, but my thirst and hunger took over, and I had guzzled over half the liter within a few seconds. "Slow down, Marlee," Ellie cautioned. "Rehydrate too quickly and you'll make yourself sick."

I nodded, remembering a time when I had rehydrated too quickly after a hot hike. That time my stomach let me know I had made a mistake – painfully and visibly! I appreciated Ellie warning me instead of me needing to dart off trail to be sick.

Meanwhile, we watched from a distance as Sawyer and Marshall each sipped their electrolyte solutions. It was impressive to see how quickly it helped perk up Marshall. I was glad for the quick turnaround, but scared of what would happen in the next few hours. What we were drinking now was the last of our electrolytes. Sure, we had plenty of water with the nearby streams and our water filter, but we all knew that all water and no food, or at least electrolytes, would further weaken us. I was making every effort to ignore the dull headache threatening to take control over my positive mood. I had no doubts that the others were battling similar symptoms. Lydie was still resting, and Sawyer turned around and motioned us to come.

Ellie stood first and held out her hand to help me up. *Yikes, that half liter feels like a melon in my stomach!*

Good thing Ellie told me to slow down. I would be careful to sip the rest over the period of the next few hours.

"Since Lydie is resting and we're all perking up thanks to tape, electrolytes and God, maybe we ought to pack up and head out. We can probably load Lydie so smoothly she'll keep sleeping, and I like the idea of her being able to rest until we find help," Sawyer stated.

Marshall nodded, and I noticed his eyes looked brighter. 'Thank you,' he silently mouthed to me, and I smiled. I thanked God that Marshall told me he was wilting so we could take action before he collapsed. Thinking of God reminded me that we should really pray again. When I suggested it, Sawyer asked Marshall to lead us in prayer. I could tell that he wasn't as confident as his brother, or even Lydie, at praying aloud, but he was sincere.

"Girls, would you please pack up the first aid kit and re-gather our packs? Marshall and I will lift Lydie back onto the stretcher. Let's keep her water bottle with her for when she wakes up," Sawyer instructed.

Ellie and I returned to the bags, and I remembered that it was my turn to carry my pack and give Marshall a break by letting him carry Lydie's relatively small pack. Hoisting my pack onto my knee, and then swiveling it around to my back, I suddenly felt very small and vulnerable again. *Stay balanced. One step at a time. You can do this, Girl.* The positive voice in my head reminded me of something I would say to a sister or friend, but I had a hunch that this encouragement was from my Father. No way was I clear-headed enough right now to think of that on my own.

I carried Lydie's pack over to Marshall, who was setting Lydie's water bottle next to her elbow in the stretcher. "You sure, Marlee?" Marshall gestured to my load.

I took a deep breath and nodded. "I'll let you know when I need to switch. Thanks for carrying it this far," I smiled. Now that all the buckles were tightened, I was feeling more stable. *Just a few more hours to Mom and Dad,* I thought.

In another moment, we all had our packs on our backs and were squatted down with the ropes of the stretcher in position on our shoulders. "On three," Sawyer called, and then to make us laugh he added, "This is for you, Marsh: uno, dos, tres." We all cracked up and stood up on tres.

II

———

"How will the Search and Rescuers find us? I mean, where will they even begin looking for us?" I pondered aloud. We had been hiking again for about ten minutes, regaining a steady pace. Sawyer's limp had lessened, Marshall was continuing to look more alive, and Lydie was resting rather peacefully. We had been silent, which gave me time to think about Mom and Dad. It made me wonder about the Search and Rescue that I prayed was activated on our behalf. Were our dads a part of the group? Would they come for us in helicopters like in an action movie? Would we be in trouble for our carelessness? Dad had told me time and again that most erosion in the mountains is caused by Search and Rescue teams helping people who were not prepared – people who had made poor decisions or people who needed help. Yikes! I had never wanted to be one of 'those people.'

"I did a research project on Search and Rescue last year," Sawyer began, clearly thinking the same thing. "In our case, where our dads will figure out what we planned, they'll probably begin the search on the peak. A group of volunteers with trained dogs probably gathered this morning to plan. They decide on where we are most likely to be found. Since we had a satellite messenger, they'll be able to locate that immediately. My prayer is that when they track down our satellite messenger and see that it's buried, they'll see the information that Marlee wrote in the snow and follow our tracks and the trail until they find us. In cases where the rescuers do not have a clue where the victim is, they actually make a grid system of an entire area, and they prioritize where to search based on the likelihood of where family and friends *think* the victim would be. But, like I said, I think Dad and Mr. Forrest will have deduced pretty accurately on our whereabouts."

Ellie and I gaped at Sawyer. My simple question resulted in a textbook answer. "Interesting," I said. "You figure Dad and Mr. Caleb will suppose that we took the ridge route rather than the more traveled northern trail?" I hopefully prodded.

Sawyer tilted his head, "That's where they may lose some time in the search. Part of me thinks our dads would certainly expect us to have taken the ridge route since it's quicker,–"

"Supposed to be quicker," Ellie butted in.

"Right," continued Sawyer, "but part of me is afraid that they would figure we'd take the safer northern trail. Then again, they'll probably start the day by tracking down Dad's satellite messenger. If they start there, they won't even bother trying to guess where we are. They'll probably start searching the whole basin area with dogs. Who knows, maybe they'll even find Marshall's pack. Since we camped there and had a fire, it should only take a little while to see our message in the snow and get on our trail."

"Do you think our moms are helping in the search?" I asked.

Sawyer shrugged, "I can't think of any reason they would not join the search teams – unless they're too panicky, and the rangers are keeping them at the station," he added quietly.

That thought made me shudder. My mom, Quinn Stanley, is very strong. She can keep cool when the rest of us are freaked out. But then again, I've never seen her in a situation where all three of her children were in danger – as in totally missing. AWOL! I wasn't sure about Ms. Julia, Sawyer and Marshall's mom, either. Anytime I have been around her, she was sweet and level-headed. But, who knows how she would cope when her boys were missing in an avalanche zone?

"Should we make excess noise or do anything to attract their attention?" Ellie asked.

Sawyer thought for a moment before deciding that we should save our energy to hike efficiently. "They'll be calling our names and making themselves audible, so let's wait until we hear them. If they see our note in the snow, they'll hike up on us quickly compared to this limp pace we're maintaining."

"*If* they see the note I wrote in the snow?" Could they miss it? I had written the letters plenty large, in block letters to increase their visibility.

"It's okay, Marlee," Ellie soothed. "Sawyer's just saying that it could take them a while to find your message, especially if they're searching on foot rather than from helicopters. And there is always the possibility of a strong wind or even another avalanche wiping away what you wrote. But, like Sawyer says, they'll have dogs to their advantage. And, even at our *limp* pace," she shot an annoyed look at Sawyer when she used his word, "we could still manage to make it to the ranger station hours before dark."

Sawyer nodded in approval of her summary. "When I said limp pace, I was making fun of myself," he muttered. "You all are excelling, and I'm just sorry I'm slowing you down."

"Stay positive, Captain!" I announced.

Ellie shook her head, and with an annoyed tone said, "Seriously, Sawyer, stop beating yourself up. The negativity is driving me crazy." *Uh-oh. This sounds like the Ellie and Sawyer we've all known for years.*

"I appreciate your kindness, Ellie, but the truth is, we wouldn't be in this predicament if it weren't for me. Lydie is injured, Marshall's weak, and Marlee had a stick in her head–"

"Avalanches happen, Sawyer!" Ellie shrieked. "But look how you've handled this situation!" She was shouting, but she didn't sound angry at Sawyer. More like she was angry with how he was getting down on himself. "Don't you get it, Sawyer Miles? We *survived* an avalanche! We spent a night without the comfort of a tent and sleeping bags and are *alive*. We are hiking out *together*. We are *evacuating* Lydie. You have done a fantastic job guiding us through challenges, and yet you keep beating yourself up. We can't change the fact that we're here now. Our job now is to trust God, be smart, and keep cooperating like you and I have miraculously done for the last few days. *Please,* change your attitude and stay as strong as I know you can be," she implored.

Wow, it turns out Ellie's speech was more of a pep talk. A bit brash, I suppose, but much more positive than the typical Ellie retort.

I glanced at Sawyer, wondering how he had perceived the 'talk.'

He bit his lip, trying to hide a smile, and said, "I'll have to give you a new nickname."

"Huh?" Ellie mused.

"When we were younger and you used to yell at me all the time–"

"When did I yell at you?" Ellie yelled, making Sawyer grin.

"As I was saying before you rudely interrupted," he teased, "Marsh and I used to refer to you as Yellie."

Ellie gasped, and Marshall busted out in laughter.

"But, that pep talk was very good. Thank you, Ellie," he sincerely said with a warm smile. And then his warm smile turned into a mischievous smile.

Ellie shyly returned his smile, and then whispered, "Was I Yellie before or after I was Smelly?"

Sawyer looked down with a hurt look, as if the reminder of the Smelly incident made him feel terrible for it all over again. "You never were smelly, but hold that thought."

Hold that thought? What does he mean by that? Ellie looked just as puzzled as me by his mysterious statement. I glanced at Marshall, who seemed purposely to avoid seeing my questioning look. Before anyone could pursue the subject, Lydie stirred uncomfortably in her sleep and whimpered, "Mommy. It hurts." Marshall and I instantly looked at her, and Sawyer and Ellie tried to look over their shoulders at her. She appeared to still be asleep, but her face was now wrinkled in a painful expression. Seeing her like that brought tears to my eyes. It was heartbreaking to see anyone, much more my little sister, writhing in painful sleep.

"Honey, we're taking you to your parents right now. We're on our way to your mom and dad. Stay strong, Lydie," Sawyer gently said in a tone like an uncle would use. While his soothing words were obviously intended for Lydie, I also appreciated them. Lydie nodded, her eyes still squeezed shut, and she seemed to fall back into a more comfortable rest.

Ellie looked worriedly over her shoulder once more at Lydie, and I saw her eyes brimming with tears as she took in the condition of our usually lively sister. "We need to be thankful that she didn't go into shock when the avalanche injured her leg," Ellie said.

Sawyer wordlessly nodded, but his grim countenance told me that Lydie's injury could have been *much* worse.

"How is everyone else holding up?" Sawyer suddenly asked us.

After a moment of shoulder shrugging, Ellie spoke first, "Battling a headache that is probably due to hunger and stress. Scared for Lydie and dying to see our parents, but otherwise I feel pretty well. I just focus on not thinking about how weak I should feel right now."

Sawyer nodded and observed her for a few steps, "You seem very resilient through this. I'm glad you feel as well as you do. Marlee?"

I groaned inwardly. It was easier to feel strong when I wasn't thinking about how I actually felt. "I'm alright.

Also ignoring a headache. My legs have started to feel a little wobbly, like wet noodles. I keep focusing on one step at a time," I said.

Sawyer glanced back, "Should we slow down or take a break?"

"Maybe not yet," I shook my head, "I still feel stronger than when the stick was in my head. We need to keep going for Lydie. I want to try to go a little longer before taking another break."

Sawyer sized me up over his shoulder as he hiked, and then turning back to face the trail he firmly said, "When you need to stop, speak up."

"Thanks for asking me, Bro," Marshall teasingly piped.

"I was getting to you. Ladies first," Sawyer chuckled. "How are you, Man?"

Marshall was clearly doing better since his electrolyte replenishment. "I feel pretty strong now, since the last liter of electrolytes. But I am nervous about the next few hours. We're basically running on fumes as it is."

The next few hours? God, please bring us back before then! I prayed.

"How are you, Sawyer?" Ellie asked, nodding to his leg.

"I'm doing fair," Sawyer honestly said. "The tape has helped stabilize my leg a ton, so I think I can keep up a steady pace in that regard. I am very hungry, though, which means we have about thirty minutes until I'll be very grouchy."

"You mean you aren't already grouchy? Oh boy, what are we in for?" Ellie joked.

Sawyer was still in good humor, but then he quietly said, "I should warn you girls that when I am really hungry..."

"He turns into a real grump! Imagine 'hangry' times one hundred!" Marshall finished for him. Marshall shook his head and continued, "You'll see a new side of him, Girls. When he's hungry, he's not even the same guy. Crabbier than-"

"Thanks for that explanation, Marshall," Sawyer annoyingly said. His voice was raised a notch, and I wondered if the crabbiness was starting now.

"There's actually a scientific explanation for that," Ellie offered. "It's very normal, and in fact, marathoners experience it at about mile nineteen. It's called–"

"Marathoners?!" Marshall jabbed. "Sawyer is hardly a marathoner!" I thought Marshall was teasing, but his brother took it seriously.

"She's not saying I am a marathoner, just that everyone gets hungry and it's called–" Sawyer motioned to Ellie.

"Glycogen depletion," Ellie nervously said, as if she feared a fight over the conversation she started.

"Call it what you want, but in our house, we call

it–" Marshall was cut off by an irritated Sawyer, who shouted, "Seriously Marshall, not now!"

I had seen Sawyer hungry before at mealtimes, but this was the first time I would have seen him this hungry, as in two-days-with-practically-no-food hungry. While his reaction to Marshall's taunting surprised me, I also knew that all of us were teetering in the same state. I know I get short-tempered when I'm hungry. I figured the countdown was on for when we all would totally lose it.

Thinking maybe I should stand up for Sawyer, I said, "Actually, Marshall, I also get pretty irritable when I'm hungry. But maybe we should hold off on the teasing until we're eating."

"I agree with Marlee," Sawyer nodded appreciatively. "And besides, it's scientific," he threw Ellie a smile.

"Tapeworms are scientific," Marshall muttered.

Sawyer looked to the sky in exasperation. "Did I mention that Marshall gets obnoxious when he doesn't meet his daily quota–"

"Obnoxious?" Marshall defended. "And your moodiness isn't ob–" I loudly cleared my throat to stop Marshall from digging himself deeper into a hole. His face was red and looked offended when he turned to look at me, but I shook my head and mouthed, 'Not now.' For a second, I thought he was going to keep arguing, but thankfully, he chose to keep his thoughts to himself this time.

I actually felt bad for Marshall. I guess that is why he prefers to say nothing than to wind up in a heated discussion and cause problems. I cast a sideways glance toward him, but his head was down, and he looked embarrassed. I asked God to return peace to our group. We could not afford a meltdown. We had to keep going.

"Shhhh!" Ellie suddenly voiced.

We looked at her, and then looked around us. Seeing only the towering ponderosa pine trees, I wondered what she heard.

"I heard someone," she hopefully said. "Over here!" she shouted with such volume that Lydie jumped in her sleep. "Help! We need help!"

Quiet. Our group stopped hiking, wishing by some miracle that Ellie had heard our rescuers. Still quiet.

"Is anybody there?" Ellie hollered. "We have an injured hiker!"

Then a rustle of leaves about fifty feet away grabbed our attention. Peering through the trees, I tried to focus my eyes on anything other than trees. Then a big ball of black skittered away from us. Four pairs of shoulders fell, but my heart was racing.

Normally I am very excited to see a bear. Well, other than last night. But this time, I was completely disheartened that our potential help was a fluffy black bear searching for berries and grub.

"Good ears, Ellie," Sawyer said. "Keep listening for

help." Ellie's face reddened. "What's wrong?" Sawyer asked, as they took the initiative to resume hiking.

"I was asking for help from a bear. How embarrassing. And," she paused, then nervously stammered, "I'm glad that bear was running away from us."

I knew she was referring to the aggressive bear from last night. When I realized that the sound was a bear, my chest had tightened with fear, and even as he was running from us, it took me a few breaths to relax.

"You girls had a genuine scare last night," Sawyer acknowledged. "Are you okay now?" He glanced back and forth between Ellie and me. I nodded, feeling more confident since we were all together. Ellie on the other hand, still red in the face, bit her lip.

Still hiking, Sawyer faced her. "El," he kindly said, "do you need to stop?"

Ellie sniffed and looked straight ahead. I could hear her breathing quicken, and because I know my sister so well, I realized she was trying not to cry. Or sob. I also knew that stopping and offering a hug would upset her worse, because she would rather give a speech to 2000 people than have four people see her cry. I knew that. I knew that Ellie wanted the conversation to switch and transfer the attention away from her emotions. But how would Sawyer know that? I give him credit; he had the best of intentions. Usually a crying girl needs compassion.

"Hey, Ellie," Sawyer stopped hiking and gestured to

the group to set Lydie down. He stepped to Ellie and reached a hand toward her shoulder.

To his shock, Ellie swatted his hand and spun around, running away from us. Sawyer looked like he had touched a hot stove. Burned and startled. Feeling the need to explain, I hastily said, "She just doesn't want to cry in front of you or in front of the group. Maybe you should go after her alone."

Sawyer shook his head, and I was afraid he was giving up on my sister. I silently prayed that he would be able to forgive her. Again.

I sighed. "I'm so sorry, Sawyer. She's embarrassed to cry in front of you," I tried again.

"Why? After all we've experienced together in the last few days, why would a few tears over a terrifying encounter with an aggressive bear embarrass her?" Sawyer asked, sounding hurt and completely annoyed.

I shrugged, "Because she is afraid to be vulnerable. Because she doesn't want you to think she's weak."

Sawyer shrugged, and then said, "I just keep messing up. I'll let you go after her."

"You don't keep messing up!" I disagreed. "You have been a saint! You–"

"I have gone way out of my way to show Ellie kindness on this trip!" He countered, and then shook his head again. "That snobby girl is a moody know-it-all and if she can't let go of her over-the-top

perfectionism, there is no room for me in her life!"
Sawyer yelled.

My heart sank when his words hit me. I actually felt
the need to sit down. And then I saw Ellie's face. None
of us had noticed she was already walking back to us.
Her face, mortified and hurt, told us that she had heard
exactly what Sawyer yelled about her. My jaw dropped,
and I leaned against a nearby tree. Sawyer thrust his
hands into his sandy blond hair, obviously regretting
his words. His expression as he saw Ellie's was sheer
dismay and remorse. He sank to his left knee,
awkwardly sticking his right leg to the side, and
clenched his fists, visibly angry with himself. Looking
up at Ellie, he quickly tried to fix his wounding words.
"Ellie, I lost my temper. I don't really mean all that.
Please let me try–"

"You've said quite enough, Sawyer," Ellie interrupted.
With tears rolling down her cheeks, she quickly wiped
her face, shook her head, and coolly said, "Enough
talking. More hiking."

Sawyer's face was beet red, and he kept his eyes on
the ground. I could imagine how terrible he felt. I have
said hurtful things before, and it is an awful feeling to
know that something I said hurt another person. But
Ellie was right that we needed to keep moving. Stopping
for a conference might mend our group's ties, but the
top priority right now was Lydie.

Without a word from anyone, Sawyer stood, and the

four of us squatted down to lift Lydie. She stirred again and sleepily asked how close to the ranger station we were. Sawyer kept his mouth shut and his eyes focused on the trail ahead. Marshall finally responded by saying, "We think we're about two hours away. You're doing just fine, Lydie. Try to drink some of your water bottle now. How do you feel?"

Lydie weakly said, "Okay, I guess," before sipping from her water bottle.

12

___

I was painfully aware of the pressure of the rope on my shoulders. It wasn't so much the weight that hurt, but the friction of the rope and the sweatshirt pressing against my shoulders. How much longer could I go on? How much longer until we would arrive at the ranger station? Where in the world were the rescuers? Surely they should have caught up to us. They must not have begun searching in the right place. What were they thinking? They were wasting precious time as our energy was waning. Ugh, what were *we* thinking? This whole mess was our fault.

Like a clap of thunder in the dark, I was suddenly reminded of a verse my mom often summarizes when I'm stressed out: "Whatever things are praiseworthy, think on these." What a reminder. Berating myself and focusing on the negative would not help.

Just a few more steps, I told myself, changing my mantra. Just a few more steps. Hopefully changing my self-talk would therefore change my attitude.

Out of nowhere, Lydie's stretcher slipped and I stumbled over her. "Owie!" she exclaimed as I landed on her injured leg. What had happened? I was weak. Very weak. Sawyer and Ellie turned around and Marshall gently set down his corner and stepped toward me. I must have unknowingly let the rope slide through my hands. I had dropped my sister! Letting my guard down had allowed negative thoughts to seep into my mind, and I had dropped my already-injured sister! A sob burst from me as I thought about this newest roadblock. Lydie groaned.

Sawyer and Marshall lifted me off Lydie and set me on the dirt ground. Sawyer and Ellie then rushed to Lydie, so Marshall began checking on me. I leaned back, propped on my elbows.

"Does anything hurt, Marlee?" he began.

I squinted at him. *When did the sun get so bright?* I wondered. My head felt a balloon. Light and unsteady.

Marshall leaned closer to me, intent on my eyes. "Marlee, does anything hurt?"

"My head." It came out as a whisper. It took so much energy to speak.

I was tuned into the sound of Lydie's groaning a few

feet away. I was aware of Sawyer and Ellie arguing about what to do next. It sounded like Sawyer wanted us to continue to stick together, but Ellie thought that two strong hikers should move on alone in search of help.

"Enough bickering!" Marshall gruffly said.

"Marlee is ready to faint and you two are just quarrelling away all your energy!" Marshall pleaded.

Apparently his appeal grabbed their attention, because in a moment, six eyes were focused on me. Sawyer touched my shoulders, and asked if I could see him. Ellie instructed the others to help slowly lower me down onto my left side. When I felt the sun-warmed ground beneath my weary shoulder, I let out a big sigh. What I would give to sleep. And eat. "Just focus on breathing, Marlee," Ellie shushed me.

Now that I was off my feet, I noticed how exhausted they were. Since we slept outside last night, we had had to keep our boots on. Though I love my hiking boots, they are restrictive, and nothing feels as good as taking them off at the end of a day on trail. What I would give to let my feet breathe, to let my muscles relax. To eat. To sleep. A tear rolled down my cheek, but nobody noticed. They were planning.

"I say we stay here and wait for the rescuers. We need to stay together," Sawyer calmly explained.

"Obviously they're not looking in the right place or they would have found us by now," Ellie countered. "I say you two guys keep heading toward the ranger station. That way I'll be with my sisters, and you can tell the rangers exactly where we are."

With my eyes shut, I could picture Marshall's disgusted expression as he told Ellie that he needed a break and wasn't up to much more hiking.

"Splitting up at this point is not wise," Sawyer stated.

"Seriously, where are the rescuers?" Ellie cut to the point. I heard her gasp and then ask, "What if they got injured? And it's our fault? And then tons of people need help, except the rescuers need help too, so who will help any of us?"

I opened my eyes at that. I couldn't find the energy to sit up, but I saw Ellie's worried face. I saw Sawyer shake his head and I heard him assure her that the terrible scenario she envisioned was extremely unlikely. She wasn't convinced. I could feel my pulse in my head.

"Ellie, even if that happened, God will never leave us or forsake us. Think about all the good things that have happened. We're all alive. The injuries we do have are relatively manageable. The weather has been ideal." He paused and then quietly said, "We need a group prayer."

He lowered his voice and calmly prayed. He thanked God for our safety and progress and asked for a prompt rescue. He asked for strength, and after he said amen, I slowly opened my eyes. I hadn't seen it before, but now I vaguely saw a small building behind the trees. *Weird,* I thought. It's strange what fatigue and hunger can do to a mind. The thought that I was seeing imaginary things scared me, so I closed my eyes again.

Sawyer leaned down to check on me. I felt mostly asleep as he shook my shoulder. Maybe I had dreamt the sight of a building in the near distance. I dared another peek, and it was still there. I continued to try to focus my eyes on it when I noticed Sawyer studying me with concern. "What is that?" I asked. But I wasn't loud enough. He didn't hear me.

"What did you say, Marlee?" he asked.

"I see something," I finally managed an audible tone. Sawyer's eyes shot up to survey our surroundings.

"Ellie, wait here. Marsh, come with me," Sawyer quickly ordered.

"Oh, so now it's a good idea to split up?" Ellie loudly asked, her tone dripping with sarcasm.

I was just hopeful that I wasn't going crazy. Sawyer must have seen it too for him to leap up on his aching leg. The boys trod down the trail about a hundred feet.

"Woohoo! Praise God!" Marshall's voice boomed through the forest.

"Girls, we're here!" Sawyer had never sounded so thrilled. "We made it! It's the ranger station!"

This roused me, and I sat up and squinted to see through the trees. Lydie propped herself up on her elbows, and Ellie jumped to her feet and let out a whoop.

The boys jogged the remaining hundred or so feet

to the ranger station and let themselves in the door. I knew enough to expect a stationary radio to be inside, even if there was no ranger in the building. Surely the radio would be set to the same channel as the radios carried by the Search and Rescue team. Sawyer and Marshall could send out a call that we were at the station. I felt a wave of comfort knowing God had carried us here! We were an enormous step closer to being with Dad and Mom and to getting Lydie to a doctor.

Three minutes later, the boys returned to us with beaming faces. "I talked to your dad," Sawyer announced, his breathing quick and shallow. "He doesn't sound like he's going to hate me for this. Two of the rescue teams are very close and will be here in probably ten minutes. The rest are looking back in the direction of where we camped the night we began our–" he paused. "Adventure," Ellie finished with a smile. Sawyer matched her smile, and then he looked emotional as he clapped Marshall's shoulder and lowered his gaze to the ground.

"Ten minutes?" Ellie's now calm tone echoed my thoughts. Ten minutes until Dad would be with us.

"Are all of our parents safe and accounted for?" Ellie asked my next thought.

Sawyer nodded, still looking at the ground. Marshall pressed his back against a tree, looking more confident than I had ever seen. Sawyer quietly explained, "Each of our parents headed up a search group. Sixteen people and two dogs have been out here searching for us."

Sixteen. Wow. I read that when a sinner returns to God, there is joy in heaven. I had an exciting feeling that this was an earthly example of that. From the silence and thoughtful faces in our group, I guessed we were all thinking similar thoughts.

Sawyer sniffed. "I'm so sorry," he plainly said.

Was Sawyer actually crying? Not that I blamed him. I was just surprised. Usually he was Mr. Calm and Collected – unless objects were being thrown at him or Ellie was being Yellie at him.

"No need to be sorry, Sawyer. We had a pretty great trek," Marshall said.

Lydie and I voiced our gratefulness for his leadership and expertise. He smiled at each of us, but didn't look proud of himself.

Ellie walked right up to Sawyer and without a word, took his hand. She held his gaze and eloquently said, "Sawyer Miles, you are an excellent guide. And you led us on a daring journey. You handled the dilemmas like a pro, and you took care of us all. Thank you for a perfect moonlit hike."

We were all shocked. Was Ellie genuine? I thought so, but for a moment I feared that she was being sarcastic. But she was still holding his hand, and she looked sincere. I admired how she strategically used the word perfect, considering Sawyer's recent announcement of her perfectionism. It was like antivenin for the tension in our group. And they were so cute holding hands like that. Sawyer's face showed that her gracious speech had finally convinced him to stop belittling himself for this whole predicament.

Sawyer and Ellie were still holding hands when we heard Dad's familiar, strong voice. "My girls! Oh, thank You, God! And my best friend's sons!"

"Daddy!" Our three voices called as he raced to us. My faintness was forgotten as I stood up and dashed toward my dad's open arms. I scarcely noticed the other three men in Dad's team. One of them began making radio calls, while the other two began taking notes and asking Lydie about her leg.

Dad looked overwhelmed as he eyed each of us, pure gratefulness in his face. His hands were shaking, and he fell to his knees thanking God. Shakily standing back up, he wrapped his arms around me and buried his whiskered face in my hair, all sweaty and matted. I felt safe and comfortable in Daddy's arms. Smelling his familiar scent gave me a sob. "Marlee," he whispered, before pulling back to look at my face. My eyes were full of tears, but through the blur I saw his hand gently reach up to peel back a corner of my gauze and check on my forehead gash. I winced at his touch on my forehead, but he murmured that it looked clean. Planting a kiss on my cheek, he looked to my sisters.

Ellie was next in line and Dad obviously noticed, but

did not say anything, as Sawyer dropped Ellie's hand so she could throw her arms around Dad's neck. He curled his arms around her waist, and as tears slid down my cheeks, I could see that Dad, too, was crying. After a hug, he held her face in his hands and gazed at her the way a new dad looks at his tiny baby. He turned to Sawyer and pulled his head into his shoulder for a man-type hug, and simultaneously gave Marshall a smile. "Your mom is going to breathe again when she sees you two," Dad said before turning to Lydie.

Crouching down to Lydie, whose eyes looked more alert than they had all day, Dad let out a huffing sound of sadness mixed with gladness. He addressed the two members of the search party who were evaluating Lydie, "May I hold her?"

One of the guys, who evidently was a wilderness medic, shook his head sternly and said that Lydie needed to stay immobile for further evaluation. The other guy elbowed him and said, just as sternly, "He's her father who didn't know if he'd ever see her again. Let him hold her."

Dad tenderly scooped her up and held her tight. "My Lydia Joy," he whispered. Lydie relaxed into Dad's chest, wearing the same relieved expression as Ellie. My heart was singing as I savored this moment of cheer.

Still holding Lydie, Dad murmured a prayer of thanksgiving. Seeming more composed now, he raised his head and grinned, "I brought food. You need to eat," he said with a slow shake of his head as he carefully observed each of us. "Honey," he addressed Lydie, "I need to set you down to get the food out of my pack."

Dad squatted down and Sawyer helped ease Lydie back onto the stretcher. "Nice work, Miles," Dad nodded to Sawyer. "Your stretcher is textbook-worthy." The medics agreed that it was the ideal setup for the situation. They said it had been 'well implemented.' Sawyer's eyes shone from the compliment. The medics continued applying pressure to Lydie's leg and asking her pain level when they held her leg in various positions.

The third man on the rescue team, who had been on the radio all the while, turned to me and began asking about my forehead. As he put on a pair of rubber gloves, Sawyer joined us and helped me answer the questions, especially about how the gash had been treated up to this point. Marshall, Ellie and Sawyer were each given short evaluations from the medics as well, but most of the attention was on Lydie.

Dad efficiently whipped up some trail pizzas for us, explaining that our bodies desperately needed the sodium before we could continue, even though we were practically at the ranger station. All the while, he just kept gazing at each of us girls, whispering our names with pride.

Over the next few minutes, Dad explained that radio calls had gone out to the other three rescue teams to alert them that we had been found. The search was called off, and all the rescuers would meet at the ranger station. Our four parents, four rangers, and eight volunteers from the mountainous community had helped to find us.

Finally, one of the men with Dad spoke up in an authoritative voice, introducing himself as Eric. "Typically the groups we rescue do not possess adequate gear or knowledge. From what I have seen of you five, I am highly impressed with your level of skill in the mountains."

Dad cut in with a shrug and a grin, "They take after Caleb and me." We snickered.

Eric smiled, but returned his attention to us kids. "Please tell me how you managed so well in this environment and under these circumstances." With an exaggerated look toward the peak in the background, he added somberly, "Most avalanche survivors at this elevation would likely have suffered severe hypothermia overnight and never made it down the mountain."

Whoa! Seriously? MOST people would have DIED? I had a feeling it would take a long time for the weight of that fact to sink in. How would I ever thank God enough for rescuing us? Glancing at our group, I realized that Sawyer and Ellie were the only ones who had considered how close to a catastrophe we had been.

We three youngest kids looked shocked and horrified; Sawyer and Ellie looked solemn.

My hands were trembling now. Probably due to the overwhelming emotion of being with Dad, rescued and ready to eat. And due to learning that statistically we were pretty much goners.

Sawyer was the first to speak up. "Sir, I mean, Mr. Eric, we believe it is a miracle that we made it through the avalanche. Being raised by professional backpackers certainly gave us an advantage in regards to experience and being equipped with the appropriate gear. But, through it all, God protected us."

Well said, Sawyer, I thought. Eric thoughtfully rubbed his chin and told Sawyer to remember what he had just said, as he might be asked to report to the newspaper, and probably the news. Sawyer nodded.

"My turn to ask a question," Sawyer said. All heads turned to him. "How did you find us?"

Dad grinned, and the other three guys raised their eyebrows, as if surprised that Sawyer had to ask.

Eric answered first, "Well, naturally we began the search by tracking your satellite messenger. Up to that point, nobody even knew the avalanche had occurred on the peak, except you, of course. When we realized it was buried in the snow, we initially feared the worst." Dad lowered his head. Eric continued, "But our dogs insisted on tracking lower. So we sent two groups lower and sent two groups back toward the direction you came the last night you were with your parents, just to cover all the bases. Amazingly the lower search teams saw your message in the snow, along with the remains of a snow shelter and fire."

"Seeing that stoked my hope," Dad quietly said.

Suddenly I heard Caleb's voice bellow out, "They're here?"

"We're here, Dad!" Marshall called as he jogged toward the direction of his dad's voice. When they met, Caleb gripped Marshall, who stood six inches shorter than his dad's tall frame, into a hug that looked like it would have forced all the air of Marshall's lungs. Marshall ducked his head into his dad's chest and squeezed his eyes shut. I walked to Dad, who was finishing up with the first pizza. Since he could only make one pizza at a time, he began to cut the finished one into five pieces which he passed out to us. I was hungry enough to swallow my slice whole, but I knew that eating slowly at first would help us to not get sick. Obviously I wasn't the only one this hungry. I glanced around and saw that the boys had pretty much swallowed their slices in a bite. Okay then. I dove in, and wow, it tasted good. All three bites.

Squatted by his stove, Dad squeezed another serving of crust batter out of a bag onto the round six-inch pan above the flame. He beamed up at me and wrapped an arm around my knees. I looked up and watched Sawyer meet his dad and join the embrace. Seeing their reunion sparked my emotions again, and I collapsed into my dad's strong arms. "Honey, honey, we're together now. And we'll be with your mom within two hours. Her group and Julia's group are hiking to us right now. Marlee, honey, I'm here," Dad hushed me. Hearing his voice after the past two days was the best music ever. He quickly spread sauce and cheese on the crust and set the lid on the pan.

A few minutes later he lifted the lid and slid his spatula under the crust, lifting the pizza onto a plate. He cut it and stood to distribute more pieces of pizza to each of us kids. We sat in a circle on the trail, Caleb asked a quick blessing (better late than never), and we continued to eat like hungry bears in the spring. Meanwhile Caleb prepared electrolyte-laden water bottles for us, which we gulped down easily.

Eric tentatively asked if we felt ready to hike the remaining tenth of a mile to the ranger station to meet our moms. We all nodded and Ellie piped, "This should be nothing now that we ate!"

Everybody laughed, and Dad, Caleb, Eric and one of the other rescuers each rushed to a corner to lift Lydie with ease. Somehow seeing our rescuers, even Dad and Caleb, ready to carry Lydie the remainder of the distance made me feel weird. It just wasn't right. As if echoing my thoughts, Sawyer suddenly commanded, "Wait!" Everyone stopped. Sawyer went on, "We should carry Lydie on the homestretch. We evacuated her this far, let's finish strong – finish as the group we started."

Dad and Caleb looked at us kids. Marshall, Ellie, Sawyer and I exchanged looks. Sure it would be easier to accept their help, but I agreed with Sawyer. Lydie cheerily voiced, "I'd offer to walk myself, but–"

"You will be carried, young lady," the main medic announced. Lydie giggled and nodded.

"I'm in," Marshall announced.

Ellie stepped toward Lydie's stretcher, "I agree." Dad and Caleb looked surprised that Ellie agreed with Sawyer, and they began looking back and forth between Sawyer and Ellie, who blushed. She rolled her eyes and quickly stammered, "This doesn't mean you're right, Sawyer. It just means that, whatever, I'm in, too."

Sawyer grinned at Ellie, and I returned to my corner of the stretcher. Dad and Caleb backed up and agreed, even though they were clearly itching to help. The other six men also allowed us to carry her, although the lead wilderness medic looked concerned.

"That's the spirit, boys!" Caleb cheered his sons. "And girls!" he added with a grin at Ellie and me. As we once again found our rhythm, I felt at ease. By now, my shoulders were numb to the pressure of the rope, and my legs were accustomed to the weight. Not appreciative of the weight, but used to it. It was not comfortable; but somehow, just knowing we were rescued and so close allowed me to ignore the physical discomforts and enjoy what we five kids had accomplished out in the wild mountains.

The sun warmed my face, and I could hear Dad's voice just a few feet behind me. Such simple, ordinary parts of life seemed so nurturing in light of the previous two days. I wondered why I had never before taken such delight in Dad's voice – or fully noticed how the sun makes nature glow. This day had turned out to be extra beautiful, especially when I viewed it through a rejuvenated perspective.

13

——

I sank into Mom's loving embrace and decided to memorize the moment and remember it forever. I have a jar at home where I keep slips of paper with special memories written. This moment, and the moment when I hugged Dad, would for sure be going in the jar. So would the sight of the peak that we almost made it to as it shone in the moonlight and the shooting star!

Mom was so overjoyed and overwhelmed with two days' worth of emotions that she was speechless. Her hug and tears on my hair said enough. After our grand reunion, Lydie was taken to the closest clinic where the doctor confirmed that there was a break in one of the bones of her lower left leg. He praised the splint and evacuation, and said that she could have needed surgery. However, since her leg had been kept so stable, the doctor was able to reset her leg in the office, and he was confident it would heal well. I'd say that was yet another miracle, without a doubt!

After waiting at the clinic a couple hours for observation, all nine of us went to a restaurant. We weren't showered or even in clean clothes, but we eagerly sat down at the local Mexican restaurant, per Marshall's pleas, as if we were royalty.

Lydie's crutches were propped against the wall, we were all in our hiking boots, and our sweat-matted hair was pretty messy. Apparently we stood out, and either we spoke loudly or our story had gained some local fame, because before our food arrived a newspaper reporter politely asked if he could interview us for the local paper.

Sawyer and Ellie did most of the talking to the journalist. Mom put one arm around Lydie and her other arm around me and whispered how grateful she was to have us back. Marshall had asked the waitress if he could keep looking at a menu even after we ordered. He needed inspiration to dream, he had said. Everyone laughed, but we kids laughed the hardest about his love for Mexican food.

"Dad," he said, completely oblivious to the journalist, "we should order some fried ice cream."

I giggled, and Caleb looked bemused. Shaking his head, he lightly flicked Marshall's menu, which made Marshall look up with a start.

"Marshall," Caleb said with a tone that suggested he was annoyed with his son's standoffish behavior. "Yesterday at this time we thought you might be gone. Really gone. Dead. We were in shock and devastated." He paused, letting his words sink in.

Marshall cautiously held his dad's gaze, and slowly nodded. Caleb continued, "I'm thrilled beyond belief that all nine of us are sitting at this table safe and healthy. I'm glad that your appetite is raging. I'm happy to feed you all night. Please pay your mom and me some attention, Marshall. Put the menu down and mentally check in to the present. You know, be here. For real."

Marshall blushed and lowered his gaze. "When you put it that way, I guess I have been pretty absent-minded," he admitted. "I guess I didn't think about how you and mom felt when we were gone. Since I knew we were safe and together, and Lydie's condition was stable, I was thankful for how we fared, but I didn't consider what you all thought based on the satellite messenger. Sorry, Dad." Caleb smiled.

"One more thing," Marshall added and Caleb gave a warm expression, summoning the usually-quiet Marshall to keep talking. "I was extremely embarrassed to have lost my pack. Just ask Marlee," he gestured at me, and I gave a knowing nod, remembering our conversation when he and I tried to reach the ranger station on our own. "When I unbuckled my pack, it was for survival. I was terrified and in that instant with the wave of white crashing toward me, I wasn't sure I had a chance at all. So I dumped my pack." Marshall looked down, still ashamed. A moment of silence, and he went on, "Then after it roared past, I didn't see anyone else in the group. I thought I was all alone without a pack, without my brother, without my parents, and without any pretty girls to keep me company."

Everybody was surprised to hear Marshall talk about girls, but we appreciated the comic relief as we listened to Marshall's emotional memory.

"This whole time, I've felt like a failure. Everybody else survived with their packs on their backs. If I'd kept it on, you wouldn't have had to think we were still buried. We would have had food. You would have found us way sooner." Marshall actually had a tear threatening to roll out of his eye. Our moms were already crying.

Caleb walked over to Marshall and put an arm around his shoulders as he squatted to his eye level. "Marshall, look at me." Marshall met his dad's eye contact. "Playing the 'what-if' game is an endless cycle that will only make you second-guess every decision. Your pack is replaceable. You made it out alive and unharmed, and that is what matters. Your backpack is gone, but you're here. It is a miracle you all survived." Marshall still looked glum. "Where is your pack now, Marsh?" Caleb questioned.

"Lost out in the snow. All that valuable gear is gone.

Including your expensive satellite messenger," Marshall annoyingly answered.

Caleb nodded, "And that is exactly where you could be too. You know, often we need to make split-second decisions. Frankly, whether or not to keep a traditional backpack on in an avalanche is debatable. Some say it'll protect your body, and that large debris rises to the surface. Others say a backpack will drag you down deeper into the snow. Obviously I'm not talking about avalanche airbag packs here. We don't always know what the best decision is. I'd say this time, since your pack is gone and you're here, you made the right decision." At that, Caleb gripped Marshall in a firm hug and cried softly into his son's hair. The emotions of the moment made me lean toward my mom and rest my head on her shoulder. She tightened her hold on my shoulders.

By now, the journalist paused his interview with Sawyer and Ellie. For a second he looked like he was tempted to turn his voice recorder toward Marshall, but he apparently decided that this part of the rescue was too emotional, too raw, too real to be in the headlines, and he clicked off the recorder on his phone and slipped it in his pocket.

After another minute, Caleb and Marshall composed themselves. The journalist shook each of our hands, asked us our names and ages and hometowns, took down a few more notes, and excused himself.

We were silent for a moment, each simply exchanging glances, smiling gratefully at each other. Lydie broke the silence, as usual. "Mr. and Mrs. Miles," she addressed Caleb and Julia. "Yes, dear?" Julia smiled at Lydie.

"How often does your family eat Mexican food?" Lydie innocently asked. Sawyer, Marshall, Ellie and I burst into laughter, but Lydie maintained a neutral expression. Dad and Mom gave me a questioning look, and I playfully rolled my eyes in response.

Caleb and Julia looked back and forth between the five of us with curious eyes, and finally, Julia cleared her throat, shrugged, and answered, "Maybe once every month or so we make tacos or enchiladas for supper. Why do you ask, Lydie?"

"Oh, just curious," Lydie said, again in that goofy innocent voice. "It was a good choice to take us to this restaurant. Some of my memories from the last two days are a bit hazy, but I vividly recall lots of talk about Mexican food."

Finally Marshall spoke up, "Nobody disagreed with me that a table-full of Mexican food would have been splendid up on that trail!"

"*Any* food would have been splendid," Lydie countered with a tease in her voice. Now our parents were laughing, too. The waitress delivered our meals just then, and I laughed when she set not one, not two, but three plates in front of Marshall. When he noticed our stares, he shrugged and said, "I'm hungry."

Warm food never tasted so good, although the increasing busyness of the restaurant began to bother me. I was oh-so thankful to be back with our families, but I looked forward to being back in nature. After an hour of slightly-heated discussion, it was finally agreed upon that we could camp tonight. My parents thought that with Lydie's broken leg, we should rent a hotel room for our last night in Colorado before beginning the drive home tomorrow. Lydie begged to camp and rattled off umpteen reasons why we should not even consider a hotel.

"I can't sleep in hotels. They're noisy," she said. "With a broken limb, sleep is crucial. I sleep best in the wilderness." Mom looked partially convinced.

"We came to backpack. If we wanted to stay in a hotel, we could have stayed seven miles from home." At that, Dad halfway nodded his head.

"But you and Sawyer need to regularly ice your injuries, as the doctors explained, and hotels have free ice," Dad stated.

"Gas stations affordably sell bags of ice. Don't let my injury ruin the trip for the Miles family, or for me," Lydie said with a mock pout-lip. Dad and Mom exchanged a glance.

Caleb laughed and Julia said, "I don't think it would be bad parenting to spend one more night in the tents.

Unloading at a hotel would be about the same amount of work as setting up camp. And she has a good point about sleep."

"And with my leg in a cast, I can't swim anyway, and everybody knows that a swimming pool is the only reason to stay in a hotel," Lydie proclaimed.

We shook our heads and laughed at her candid reasoning. I was secretly very glad that we would be able to camp once more. Being immersed in nature is such a rich experience. Because it was now close to dusk, and hiking was obviously out, we chose to find a mountain meadow very nearby to set up our final camp.

As we drove onto the gravel trail where we could easily access the site, the sun was glowing orange-pink in the west. The air smelled pure, and I could hear songbirds. I sighed happily. Mom helped Lydie situate an ice bag on her leg, and Sawyer casually placed an ice bag on his lower leg, too. Seeing Mom with Lydie made my heart bubble with joy.

As all nine of us sat in a circle for our traditional end-of-day talk, I felt a genuine contentment wash over me. I loved our adventure, but it sure was good to be with the familiar routine again!

"I have to ask," Dad looked at us kids, "how was the view?" We knew without explanation that he was referring to the view from the peak during the full-moon summit.

All five of us nodded, trying to remember back two

nights ago. In a way it seemed much longer ago than two nights. "It was going to be perfect," Sawyer wistfully said.

"What we saw *was* perfect," Ellie reminded him.

"We were at the last false summit, and it's a good thing we stopped to enjoy the view there," Sawyer recalled. "We figured we had one hour to go before we stood on top."

"And then we heard a roar," Marshall added.

"And Marshall yelled to try to swim," I said. "And a wild minute later, all I saw was black."

Dad and Caleb looked serious, and Mom looked like she might get sick. Julia didn't look much better.

"We'll come back to this story," Sawyer said, realizing that the memory was too fresh, the fear too strong, to discuss now. "Next question is for Mr. Stanley," Sawyer looked squarely at Dad. I gulped. Ellie looked curious and shy.

"Forrest," Dad said, "You can call me Mr. Forrest."

Sawyer nodded, "That's what I don't get. If I had daughters who snuck off with some guy on a crazy adventure that was potentially deadly, I would resent and despise the guy. How are you not furious with me?" He plainly, and I thought quite bravely, asked.

Dad sucked in a breath, and for a second his jaw tightened, which happens when he is upset. He looked thoughtful, and Sawyer looked nervous for his response. Finally Dad let out a breath, looked right at

Sawyer, and slowly answered, "First of all, you're not some guy. You are Sawyer Miles, you are my best friend's son whom I have known and liked all your life. You are trustworthy, experienced, and your sense of adventure reminds me of your dad and me. At first I was upset. Furious, even. When I saw my girls' tent empty, in that moment, I could have reamed you out. Taking my girls, in the dark, not so much as leaving a note with your plan – that all made me mad. But I knew that my girls would not have gone with you unless they wanted to go, so the anger wasn't exclusively targeted at you. When you didn't return when we assumed you'd be back, the anger gave way to fear. Horrible, immense fear. After that, we were all in shock as we began to initiate the search." Dad paused, deep in thought.

Still looking at Sawyer, he continued, "I'll tell you this, Sawyer: as the Search and Rescue formed and you five kids were lost, all I could think about was finding you. All of you. And praying desperately that you were all safe. I learned from this that anger needs to be low on my priority list. I could've spent the last two days thinking up my lecture for you, feeding my anger. Or I could put my energy into finding you. It didn't take me long to determine which was more important. At the end of the day, what would my anger at you accomplish?" Dad waited a moment for us to think about what he'd said. I was impressed with this long monologue. We remained quiet.

"Sawyer, I'm not mad at you. Nor am I angry with any of you kids. Honestly, I can't even say that I'm disappointed with what you did. Now," his voice suddenly was stern, "next time, you'll leave us a written plan of your itinerary." We all nodded solemnly. Dad's voice softened, and he continued, "I can see why you didn't tell us what you planned to do. You were right to assume that we probably would not have allowed you to go alone. *But,* had you asked us, we would have gone along, so you would have been allowed to go."

I knew it! We could have had our dads with us the whole time.

"Of course that's not to say that in that instance all of us would have been in the avalanche, and who can say how that would have turned out. The outcome of this is a tremendous blessing. But getting back to the point, I can understand why you didn't ask permission to go, but as a professional guide, you will be expected to always leave a detailed itinerary, and as a man with sense, you will do that from now on," Dad instructed Sawyer.

"Yes, sir," Sawyer respectfully replied.

"Besides," Dad said in a lighter tone, "your dad and I know you don't need a lecture. This incident taught you plenty. You flirted with fire and reaped consequences." Sawyer nodded seriously.

"I echo what Forrest says," Caleb spoke up. "I felt like my heart stopped when I realized you left. But when I found your thorough packing list in the corner of your tent and saw that you had taken the satellite messenger, I was glad that you were smart about it. And like Forrest said, the longer we waited and searched, the more the anger and disappointment faded."

Our moms silently cried through the conversation. We all sensed it was time for the discussion to move on.

"Next question is from me, and it's for Sawyer and Ellie," Dad cautiously said, slowly glancing back and forth between the two of them.

Ellie blushed, and Sawyer gave her a nervous smile. They were sitting next to each other, which was an unusual happening.

"I can't help but notice," Dad gently started, "that you two don't seem to be at each other's throats lately. I just wonder if there has been a change you want to tell us about?" It was kind of awkward, Dad asking them that question, but I was glad he did. I mean, I guess I'd rather have parents who want to know who we like, even though it's a little weird to talk about. Mom knew all about Bentley and me. And then Bentley and Sierra. And it helped so much that I could talk to her. So I figured it's good that our parents know about Sawyer and Ellie. We need Dad and Mom to be involved in our lives. Everyone perked up and closely watched Sawyer and Ellie for their response. I still felt like I knew a secret since only I saw them by the fire.

Sawyer looked sort of guarded, as if he would rather

not discuss the topic in front of all of us. Ellie looked more confident, and she cleared her throat before beginning.

"Actually, Dad and Mom," she addressed our parents, "there has been a significant change, but I think you'll be pleased with it." Dad and Mom were intent on what she was about to say.

Ellie took a breath and went on, "Through all of this, I learned to respect Sawyer and to treat him well. And surprisingly," she tilted her head playfully, "I learned that Sawyer is not so terribly annoying." Dad teasingly gasped, which made Lydie and me giggle. "It turns out that Sawyer is a great friend," Ellie concluded with a grin at Sawyer. Sawyer looked happier than a climber at the peak.

Mom and Dad, as well as Caleb and Julia, looked very pleased. Marshall and I exchanged a knowing glance.

Then Sawyer began, giving Ellie an admiring look, "I learned that Ellie's strive for excellence is what makes her successful in all she does. She's definitely not the know-it-all perfectionist that I used to peg her as," he gently added, deepening Ellie's blush. Sawyer turned his gaze to Dad and, as if he'd rehearsed it a few times, said, "Maybe someday I'll work up the courage to ask your permission to ask Ellie out. On a date, I mean."

Lydie's jaw dropped, Marshall pumped his fist, and my eyes darted to see my parents' reaction. Dad looked surprised, but after a split second, he seemed very happy with Sawyer's respectful request. Mom looked startled, and almost appeared in disbelief, as if she thought it was a joke. Caleb and Julia looked proud of their son. Apparently they were not surprised at the change in attitude between Sawyer and Ellie.

Marshall spoke up now, "Marlee and Lydie and I were shocked at first with how well Sawyer and Ellie worked together on this trip. I mean there was the usual Sawyer-Ellie tension during the planning, but once we were hiking, and then especially after the avalanche, it was remarkable to see them cooperating like well-mannered citizens." This made us all laugh, and Sawyer and Ellie looked almost radiant as they smiled at each other. "Well," he added, "there was still a little squabbling, but there was also tons of what Marlee thinks is *cute*." We laughed again when he used air quotes for cute.

Still chuckling, I leaned back onto my elbows and looked at the sky as it darkened, allowing the first twinkling stars to peek at us. I sighed happily, and then smiled at Mom, who returned a genuinely happy smile.

Caleb broke the silence, "We all need our sleep now. Especially those with injuries, those recovering from emotional trauma, and those who are overtired and underfed," he said seriously.

"So, all of us," Marshall concluded.

Backpacking has taught me many life lessons, one of them being the importance of sleep. Without adequate sleep, we can't enjoy the beauty, we're not up to the challenges, and our bodies hurt! None of us argued Caleb's bedtime call. Dad had already excused himself to begin setting up tents.

Dad and Mom chose to have Lydie squeeze into their tent so they could keep a close eye on her and give her the prescribed medicine without much hassle. I loved watching Daddy scoop Lydie up into his strong arms and easily walk her to their tent. After settling her, he came back to give Ellie and me hugs.

"Your mom will come in a minute to say goodnight, but I'm going to take my sweet time enjoying you two beauties. Girls, in spite of you sneaking off without leaving a note, I want you to know that I'm proud of you both," he looked us in the eyes.

"For real?" I squeaked, still half-expecting a lecture. I mean seriously, pioneer kids would have been whipped. Dad was actually proud of us, at least partially?

Dad nodded. "I can imagine the amount of courage and endurance you had to display to do what you did. Obviously God was on your side, but nonetheless, I am proud of the way you conducted yourselves to come out of the avalanche and evacuation in such fine condition. And you took such excellent care of Lydie," Dad concluded with a smile.

"Sawyer showed us how to set up the stretcher," Ellie commented, and then blushed when we smiled at her mention of Sawyer. Dad gave us each a kiss on the forehead and reminded us to always remember the best parts of the day, as he does every night. As he walked back to his tent, I saw Caleb pull him aside to talk.

Mom came and wordlessly hugged us tight. She kissed my head and said she could never thank God enough.

Snuggling into my cozy sleeping bag next to Ellie, I breathed in the fresh mountain air and had no trouble falling into a deep sleep.

14

___

I woke up to sun glinting through the tent wall and a few early birds singing their good morning tunes. I could hear Caleb whistling, and the familiarity of his melody reminded me of past enjoyable trips. I was so glad to wake up in our tent. Faint rustling from the boys' tent indicated that Sawyer and Marshall were not quite awake. I yawned, silently thanked God for an incredibly comfortable night of sleep and then rolled over to see if Ellie was awake yet.

Ouch! As I rolled, every muscle in my body hurt. It made sense, I suppose, to have muscle soreness after two days of hiking without food. That was in addition to being tossed around in the avalanche. I wondered why I hadn't noticed the soreness until now.

Ellie giggled at my grimace and said, "Morning. Did your muscle soreness kick in, too?"

I nodded, "Evidently."

"How are you otherwise, Marlee?" she asked sincerely.

"Just extremely thankful for this happy ending," I responded with a smile. "And you?"

"Also thankful with every fiber of my being. So thankful that I'll try to overlook my sore muscles," she said, also smiling.

We crawled out of the tent and found Caleb already taking down our bear bags, ready to make us breakfast.

"I woke up with a growling stomach, so I'm glad to see you, Mr. Caleb!" I called.

"Good morning to you, too, Marlee," he laughed.

"She treats me that well, too, Dad," Marshall teased as he climbed out of his tent.

I laughed my greeting to him, and he gave a playful wink as his dad shook his head and chuckled. One by one everyone filed out of the tents, and the five of us kids looked rested, despite our aching muscles. Mom hugged me and said I looked well-rested, unlike the day before. She, too, looked like she had slept well. Lydie clumsily practiced using her crutches and did not accept help. "It already feels like I've been sitting and riding too long. If I'm going to stay strong, I need to do this myself," she said with determination.

Half an hour later, we were all gathered around the

humming camp stoves as they warmed water for oatmeal. After Caleb led us in prayer, Dad cleared his throat and asked for our attention.

"The four of us parents had a conversation last night," he started and my stomach dropped, full of sudden nerves. *Might as well get the deserved punishment over with.*

Dad must have noticed our pale, concerned faces, because he quickly added, "No need to worry. We agreed that we want the five of you to plan next summer's backpacking trip."

Sawyer perked up and beamed, and the rest of us smiled widely at our parents and at each other. *No way!* I thought. *What a privilege!* Mom nodded and smiled.

Caleb must have heard my thoughts, because he started in, "Now, as you know, with privilege comes responsibility. After what you exhibited during your moonlit hike, we realized that it's time to let out the rein, so to speak. We need to give you kids more responsibility while you're still safely in the nest. This will be an opportunity for you to take on a significant role, yet you'll have us available for advice. Questions?" He gestured to us.

"Dad, thank you!" Marshall said.

"We all decided on it," Caleb nodded to the other three adults. *Wow. They're passing on this responsibility of planning our family trips. Is this for real? We're not grounded for ten years?*

This time Dad heard my thoughts, because he spoke up, "I'm sure you realize that this is difficult for Caleb and me to let our role move on to someone else. It will be close to impossible for me to keep my nose out of your plans. But we ask that you come to us with any questions."

Mom assertively added, "And we also agreed that there are a few stipulations."

Sawyer cocked his head, "No international trips, I'm guessing?"

Dad and Caleb laughed and Julia said, "That will be added to the list of stipulations."

"As you know, we always strive to have trips planned five months beforehand, and permits obtained as soon as possible, usually four months before the start date of the trip," Caleb mentioned.

"And of course, you'll need to keep the trip within our budget," Dad added.

"And because of logistics, it needs to be no more than seven days," Mom reminded.

"And no spelunking!" Julia instructed.

We all laughed, especially Lydie, who remembered a time a few years ago when she convinced Julia, who is smaller than Mom, to wiggle into a cave with her. Lydie thoroughly enjoyed the underground adventure. Julia, on the other hand, discovered that day that she fears tight places. So caves were not an option.

Marshall piped up, "With all the great views above ground, we shouldn't need to go underground."

"Can we go to the Grand Canyon?" Lydie excitedly asked. Dad casually shrugged and said, "You'll need to discuss it with the council."

"I can't wait to start planning," Sawyer said. "Let's each prepare a list of our top five locations. Marshall and I will drive to your house next month, and we can start arranging the ninth annual Stanley-Miles backpacking trip!" Well, he was ready to plan!

At first I was surprised that we would meet in a month, but then realized that if our plans had to be finalized in six to seven months, we did need to begin soon. Ellie looked pleased that Sawyer and Marshall would make the five-hour drive to our house. I smiled as I thought back to our conversation about Sawyer prior to this trip. What a change!

Our parents approved of Sawyer's decision to start planning immediately. Usually Dad and Caleb began discussing the next year's trip before the end of summer, so I guess it made sense; although usually they did much of the planning over the phone. I suspected that Sawyer had another reason for offering to visit us in person. I still could hardly believe that he had basically told Dad that he wanted to ask Ellie on a date!

After breakfast and teeth brushing, we began to pack up our tents. As I stuffed my sleeping bag into its tiny compression bag, my shoulders ached again, reminding me of the miles we carried my sister. I had a hunch that I would still be learning life lessons from this trip for many years.

Ellie was beside me in the tent, on her knees, filling her pack. Suddenly I heard Sawyer's voice at our tent flap. "Ellie?" he called. Ellie jumped at hearing his voice, and then cast me a nervous expression. I gave an encouraging smile. "Yes?" she squeaked. I had to stifle a giggle at the nervous edge in her voice.

"Uh," Sawyer paused, as if unsure how to start conversation through a tent. Clearing his throat, he said, "Do you have a minute to talk?"

"Um, yeah," she said, and then sounding more certain, added, "I mean, yes. I definitely have time to talk to you."

Phew, good correction, Ellie! I thought.

I totally whispered "I told you so," and then I smiled warmly at her as she stepped out of our small tent. They walked behind our tent, about eight feet away. Conveniently, our tent flap happened to be open on that side, so I could clearly watch them through the mesh screen. I wondered if it was rude of me to listen in, but I knew that Sawyer was chaste enough to not do or say anything that needed total privacy. And really, if he didn't want me to watch and listen, he would have led her farther away. Besides, Dad would appreciate having someone chaperone. I just happened to be the most available.

Ellie faced Sawyer and curiously looked up at him. Sawyer looked nervous to proceed. The suspense was killing me! Finally he said, "I have something to give you, Ellie."

Ellie raised her eyebrows and anxiously said, "You didn't have to get me anything, Sawyer."

Sawyer scratched the back of his neck and said, "Well, uh, I mean, I didn't actually get you a gift. I'm sorry. I didn't think of that." Ellie laughed nervously, and Sawyer quickly added, "It's actually a return."

He reached into his jacket pocket and handed her something, but I couldn't see what it was. "A beautiful girl once threw this at me. But it belongs to her, and it's time I give it back." Ellie's eyes were huge as she observed Sawyer's face, and then looked at her faded green bandana in her hand. "You saved this?" she whispered, just barely loud enough for me to hear.

Sawyer nodded.

"Did you call me beautiful?"

"Um, yes, I did," Sawyer softly – and nervously – spoke.

Ellie stepped forward, and Sawyer pulled her into a hug so sweet that my face broke into a grin and I whispered, "Aww," to myself. Was this really happening? I slowly shook my head in disbelief as I watched Sawyer and Ellie hug again. After a few seconds, they stepped apart and Ellie again asked about her bandana. "What made you keep this for, what's it been, three years?"

Sawyer blushed and cautiously said, "Even though we always drove each other crazy, I, uh, couldn't bear to get rid of it. I didn't want to get rid of it. It reminded me of you, and even though I pretended that you annoyed me, I guess maybe I liked you after all. Either way, I always wanted to apologize for what I said to you. And anyway, it belongs to you."

Now Ellie blushed, then smiled, and shook her head with a little laugh. "When we were packing for this trip, Marlee was teasing me about you. I didn't want to think about you, I guess, but it turns out she was right all along." Now it was my turn to blush, even in the privacy of the tent.

Sawyer tilted his head and curiously prodded, "What was Marlee right about?"

Ellie shrugged and said, "Oh," and then trailed off, looking like she regretted bringing up this point.

Sawyer grinned and wiggled his eyebrows. "Was it," and then donning a theatrical tone, he continued, "that my ruddy good looks would finally convince you to notice my incredible personality?" I stifled a giggle. Corny. But still cute.

Ellie's blush deepened, but she played along and casually said, "That's an accurate paraphrase of what Marlee said." I could tell Sawyer was surprised with her response, because his eyebrows jumped up two inches, and he didn't say anything for another minute.

"In all seriousness, Ellie," he quietly said, "thank you for trusting me this week and for," he took a breath, "well, for being a friend." Ellie's smile could have lit up a cave.

And then I sneezed. That never happens in real life! Why would I sneeze at a moment like this? Unbelievable. Sawyer and Ellie turned to look at me with amused expressions, "Did you get the recording, Marlee?" Ellie teased as they walked to the tent together.

Sawyer popped his head in the tent doorway and followed suit, saying, "You didn't get much packing done!"

I blushed, "You two are just so, so–"

"Say it, Marlee," he said playfully.

"Cute. And compatible, and I'm relieved that you two have moved past constantly clashing," I hurriedly finished.

They each gave me a genuine smile and then shared yet another smile with each other.

"Really, think about how much easier this will make planning next year's trip now that you can be within a hundred feet of each other and not make everyone else miserable." I had to break the silence with something humorous. I was surprised with my Lydie-like comment. Sawyer and Ellie laughed and Ellie ducked into the tent to resume packing while Sawyer headed back to his tent.

After another half an hour we were all packed up. Dad and Caleb used their hiking boots to gently fluff up the grass where we had camped. I was glad to have been taught strict adherence to leaving no trace, even though it sometimes seemed a bit over the top, like fluffing up grass.

Glancing at our stuffed vehicle, I thought about how odd it was that five people could carry enough gear to fill a vehicle completely. Considering how sore my body felt, I knew it wasn't easy, but certainly possible.

Dad and Caleb shook hands and pulled each other close for a sort of one-sided man hug. Mom and Julia hugged, and we kids exchanged brief hugs before our departure.

"See you girls next month for planning," Marshall said as he hugged Lydie and me at the same time. "Take care of that leg, Lydie," he added. "Marlee, thanks again for talking sense into me."

I smiled and nodded, and typically-witty Lydie beat me to the punch line, "Well, she made a start. Of course, it will take several more sessions to really have you thinking sensibly."

Marshall chuckled and I said, "Thank you for sharing that information about guys." He nodded, and Dad protectively interrupted, "I, too, will be interested to hear the information about guys on the car ride." Dad shot me a curious look.

"It's nothing bad, Dad. Marshall just gave me some pointers on how to treat guys respectfully, like brothers."

Dad nodded without looking fully convinced. "You kids did have an enormous adventure, didn't you?" Dad said after a thoughtful moment.

Lydie, Marshall and I nodded with large eyes. "I'm kind of jealous I missed out. But happy with how it ended. And I want to hear all about it," Dad concluded.

Extending his hand for Marshall to shake, Dad said, "I look forward to hearing how the planning progresses." Marshall nodded and smiled before Dad stepped toward Sawyer who was flirting with Ellie.

"You're a fine young man, Sawyer. Anytime you need to talk about backpacking, trip planning, wilderness rescue, or my beautiful daughter, I'll be ready to listen," Dad said.

"Thank you, Mr. Forrest," Sawyer made eye contact with Dad, and they shook hands.

As we loaded into our vehicles with the bright blue sky above us and the elusive peak filling the horizon, I felt my eyes fill with tears. I love home, and it would be good to return to running water and indoor plumbing, but our time in the wild always seems too short. As we pulled out of the meadow and exchanged final waves with the Miles family, I was especially glad that we

206 · M. Liz Boyle

would be meeting with the boys in a month to plan our next adventure together. As eventful as the last week had been, I somehow had an empty feeling in my gut. I could not escape the feeling that we didn't fully accomplish what we set out to do. Dad talks about some hikers being goal-oriented, who will take unwise risks just to make it to the peak. On the contrary, other hikers are experience-oriented, and regardless of whether they achieve the summit, they find joy in the experience.

I'm not sure into which category I fit. I mean, we experienced so much this week, and the skills I learned are invaluable. I am thankful for all that I managed to do, and though it seems strange, I am glad for the opportunity to have pushed myself in such a challenging environment. I think I worked harder in those two days than in all my life – physically and mentally! And spiritually – never have I had to rely on God more fully than when I was covered in snow, contending with pain to keep up with Marshall, and fighting hunger and cold to sleep under the glittery stars. Looking back on the satisfaction acquired from these experiences, I started to think maybe I am experience-oriented.

But, as I watched that big, dangerous summit shrink and finally fade from sight after two hours of driving, I wondered if maybe I am goal-oriented. I admitted to myself that we hadn't completed our adventure. We set out to see the view from the summit in the moonlight, and though we did get close, it bothered me that we missed out on the sight we risked so much to see.

My eyelids grew heavy, and I sighed into an exhausted sleep, finding comfort that adventure is everywhere. And, no matter where the next adventure in life lies, I'll have God on my side. That alone makes every day meaningful. So whether I'm climbing a mountain or weeding the neighbor's garden, each moment is an opportunity to achieve greatness with God.

And I knew right then where I would suggest to the group that we go next summer.

Epilogue

"They're here!" Lydie announced, barely limping in her walking boot to open the door. Ellie dodged past Mom into the bathroom *again* to check her hair and the dash of eye shadow she had applied.

"Come on, Ellie!" I moaned. "Sawyer has seen you look filthy and all messy and he knows you're beautiful anyway. You look ten times better than you normally look around him!" Mom laughed and winked at me.

Ellie ignored my comment and quickly tucked a strand of her dark hair behind her ear before rushing to the door. Lydie had already let Sawyer and Marshall into the entryway and they were raving over the condition of her left leg. "Look at that range of motion," Sawyer noted as Lydie showed off some of her physical therapy exercises. Lydie beamed.

"It doesn't even hurt anymore?" Marshall wondered.

"Hi, guys!" I exclaimed, happy to see our trail buddies again.

They looked up, and Sawyer's eyes instantly fell on Ellie's face. He smiled warmly and Ellie returned the expression. Sawyer looked really happy. I knew he had gotten a call from POGS, and they still wanted him to attend this fall, just two months from now. Last week Sawyer had turned eighteen. When POGS heard about the avalanche and how Sawyer led us, they were even more excited that their new youngest student was already so prepared and experienced.

Marshall winked at Lydie and me and then announced, "Should we roll out these topographic maps on the table? The sooner we finish the preliminary planning, the sooner we can take these girls out for tacos. What's that yummy restaurant here? Enelda's Enchiladas?"

Lydie and I burst into laughter, and at first Sawyer and Ellie seemed completely oblivious, but then Sawyer remembered the main reason they had come and said, "We don't need the topographic maps yet. Let's start by laying out our lists of top five destinations and narrowing it down to two locations. Then we'll make itineraries and figure out the costs for both proposed trips. Then we'll decide."

"And then we'll get out the topo maps," Marshall finished.

"But first, we should pray. We want this trip to be in God's hands, right from the start," Sawyer explained as we bowed our heads and he asked for God's blessing on our planning efforts.

We each sat around our dinner table and set our lists in the center, in plain view for each other to read.

My excitement bubbled inside me as I dreamed about the various locations on each of our lists. The Grand Canyon, along with peaks in Alaska, California, Washington and Wyoming were all found amongst our potential trips. Interestingly, but not surprisingly, the first location on each of our lists was the same. Apparently we all held the desire to once again try to see the view from the peak we had just left behind.

The thought of returning to the location where we came dangerously close to death was scary. But maybe we had to have victory on it before we could move on to other peaks. Just like in life, we need to overcome our fears before exploring the next adventure. And sometimes the best adventures are found in an avalanche.

Glossary of Terms

Bight (pronounced 'bite'): a loop of rope used to tie a knot

Crampons: metal attachment to the bottom of a hiker's boots with spikes to increase traction

Fourteener: a mountain peak whose height above sea level is greater than 14,000 feet; Colorado has about 58 fourteeners.

Ice Axe: T-shaped tool used in snow and ice to help climbers avoid slipping down a slope

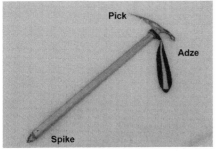

Moleskin: flexible but durable cloth with an adhesive backing used in treatment of blisters

About the Author

Photo by Krista Swanson
/ Simple Wonder Arts

Liz is an author, the wife of a professional tree climber and the mom of three energetic and laundry-producing children. She received her Associate's of Arts at the University of Sioux Falls, where she received the LAR Writing Award for her essay entitled, "My Real Life

Mufasa." Liz once spent a summer in Colorado teaching rock climbing, which she believes was a fantastic way to make money and memories. She resides with her family in Wisconsin, where they enjoy hiking and rock climbing. Liz and her husband have also backpacked in Colorado and the Grand Canyon, which have provided inspiration for her writing. She likes making adventurous stories to encourage others to find adventures and expand their comfort zones (though admittedly, she still needs lots of practice expanding her own comfort zone). She has thoroughly enjoyed working on her first novel, *Avalanche.* Stay tuned for a sequel!

For a discussion guide for *Avalanche,* please see https://mlizboyle.com/avalanche-discussion-guide/

Dear Reader,

One of the best ways to help an author is by word of mouth. If you enjoyed *Avalanche*, please tell your friends about it! Posting reviews online is another great way to help authors. The more readers that find this story, the more I can keep writing adventures for us all to enjoy!

Blessings,

Liz

Made in the USA
Las Vegas, NV
10 September 2021